The sound of a deafening crash echoed across the surface of Dantar IV. . . .

A raucous cheer went up from everyone in the cannon housing. But it was quickly stifled as they heard the sounds of sobbing and cries from the colonists outside, and the air filled with a thick cloud of black smoke.

"Worf!" called out K'Ehleyr. He went over and knelt down next to her. She was cradling the bleeding head of Professor Trump in her lap, and she looked up at Worf worriedly. "If he doesn't get medical attention immediately, I don't think he's going to make it."

"Medical attention is going to be a problem," said Dini, coming over. "The infirmary was one of the first things to be hit in the initial raid. I don't even want to think what's left of it by this point. Probably nothing."

Zak looked at Worf and said what they already knew: "We're not out of trouble yet, are we?"

Worf shook his head. "No. Not by a long shot."

Star Trek: The Next Generation
STARFLEET ACADEMY

Available from MINSTREL Books

STAR TREK
THE NEXT GENERATION™

STARFLEET ACADEMY™ #2
LINE OF FIRE

Peter David

Interior Illustrations by James Fry

A
MINSTREL®
BOOK

PUBLISHED BY POCKET BOOKS

New York   London   Toronto   Sydney   Tokyo   Singapore

This book is a work of fiction. Names, characters, places, and inci-
dents are either products of the author's imagination or are used
fictitiously. Any resemblance to actual events or locales or persons,
living or dead, is entirely coincidental.

A MINSTREL PAPERBACK ORIGINAL

A Minstrel Book published by
POCKET BOOKS, a division of Simon & Schuster Inc.
1230 Avenue of the Americas, New York, NY 10020

Copyright © 1993 by Paramount Pictures. All rights reserved.

STAR TREK is a Registered Trademark of
Paramount Pictures.

This book is published by Pocket Books, a division of
Simon & Schuster Inc., under exclusive license from
Paramount Pictures.

ISBN: 0-671-87085-8

First Minstrel Books printing October 1993

10 9 8 7 6 5 4 3 2 1

A MINSTREL BOOK and colophon are registered trademarks of
Simon & Schuster Inc.

Cover art by Catherine Huerta

Printed in the U.S.A.

To Debbie Shepperson,
Klingon Babysitter

STARFLEET TIMELINE

2264

The launch of Captain James T. Kirk's five-year mission, U.S.S. Enterprise, NCC-1701.

2292

Alliance between the Klingon Empire and the Romulan Star Empire collapses.

2293

Colonel Worf, grandfather of Worf Rozhenko, defends Captain Kirk and Doctor McCoy at their trial for the murder of Klingon chancellor Gorkon.

Khitomer Peace Conference, Klingon Empire/Federation (Star Trek VI).

2323

Jean-Luc Picard enters Starfleet Academy's standard four-year program.

2328

The Cardassian Empire annexes the Bajoran homeworld.

2341

Data enters Starfleet Academy.

2342

Beverly Crusher (née Howard) enters Starfleet Academy Medical School, an eight-year program.

2346

Romulan massacre of Klingon outpost on Khitomer.

2351

In orbit around Bajor, the Cardassians construct a space station that they will later abandon.

2353

William T. Riker and Geordi La Forge enter Starfleet Academy.

2354

Deanna Troi enters Starfleet Academy.

2356

Tasha Yar enters Starfleet Academy.

2357

Worf Rozhenko enters Starfleet Academy.

2363

Captain Jean-Luc Picard assumes command of U.S.S. Enterprise, NCC-1701-D.

2367

Wesley Crusher enters Starfleet Academy.
An uneasy truce is signed between the Cardassians and the Federation.
Borg attack at Wolf 359; First Officer Lieutenant Commander Benjamin Sisko and his son, Jake, are among the survivors.
U.S.S. Enterprise-D defeats the Borg vessel in orbit around Earth.

2369

Commander Benjamin Sisko assumes command of Deep Space Nine in orbit over Bajor.

Source: Star Trek® Chronology / Michael Okuda and Denise Okuda

LINE OF FIRE

CHAPTER

1

"Behind you!"

The two Starfleet Academy cadets shouted the same warning at the same time. For only the briefest of moments there was confusion on their respective faces, and then they came to the abrupt realization that they were each alerting the other to imminent danger.

As a result they both spun just before the lurching Zendorian warriors managed to get close enough to do harm. The two Zendorians, helmeted, towering, hairy, and not known for personal hygiene, roared defiance.

The sky overhead was a glaring red, the scalding sun having baked the ground dry ages ago. The air was thin and still. No sound could be heard except the grunts of the combatants as they battled across the plateau.

Academy Cadet Worf dropped low to the craggy ground and drove a punch toward the upper thigh of the closer Zendorian. The creature roared and fell to

one knee, and Worf seized the opportunity. He grabbed a fistful of the Zendorian's thick hair and slammed him down as hard as possible. He delivered a final blow for good measure—not to mention safety's sake—to the back of the Zendorian's head, and Worf's huge opponent did not move again.

Worf spun and saw that his partner, Zak Kebron, was still slugging it out with his own adversary. Zak was a Brikar, as strong as Worf (stronger, in Zak's opinion) although a bit slower (a lot slower, in Worf's opinion), with a tough skin (which matched his personality, in both their opinions).

Zak was taking a fierce pounding. The Zendorian was unarmed, because Zendorians felt that to strike at an opponent with anything other than bare fists was to imply weakness. A true warrior, it was felt, needed no help in defeating a foe.

Zak's hard hide barely quivered under the impact of the Zendorian's fists. And he returned the blows with equal force, not budging an inch.

The Zendorian swung a roundhouse punch, and Zak ducked under it. It threw the Zendorian slightly off balance, and that was enough for Zak to come in under his guard and slam him just under his chin. The Zendorian's head snapped back, and Zak struck once more. The quick succession of blows finally took its toll. The Zendorian, with a last squeak of defiance, pitched forward and fell with such force that the ground shook from the impact.

Worf and Zak Kebron stood there for a moment, bent

slightly forward, resting their hands on their thighs and taking quick breaths to compensate for the heat.

"That was wasteful," Worf finally managed to get out.

Zak looked at him askance. "What was?"

"We studied Zendorians in self-defense training. We learned about their weak spot right here," said Worf, tapping his own thigh in the same place that he had struck the Zendorian. "Why did you spend all that additional time engaging in a pointless struggle?"

"Pointless?" Kebron looked stunned that Worf would use the word. "There was nothing pointless about it. I proved who was the stronger."

"That was not the goal!" said Worf in annoyance. "The goal was to defeat the enemy, quickly and efficiently."

"You choose your goals, Worf," Zak retorted, "and I'll choose mine." He raised his voice slightly and said, "End simulation."

The arid world promptly blinked out of existence, along with the two unconscious Zendorians. It was replaced by the black-walled, yellow-lined grid of a holoroom.

"Our goals should be the same, Zak," Worf rumbled as they headed out the door and into one of the main corridors of the Academy. "The goal is survival, not posturing or tests of personal endurance. If you were capable of dispatching the Zendorian with greater efficiency and speed, then you should have done so."

"It was a training exercise, Worf, that's all," said Zak, making no effort to hide his impatience. "In a training exercise where it's the two of us versus the two of them, why not get in a little extra exercise?"

"What if it hadn't remained just the two of them?" Worf pointed out. "Zendorians are known for creating below-ground hideaways. We could have had a dozen more right under our feet. If more had attacked, you would have felt somewhat foolish spending the time dispatching an opponent that you could have disposed of in half the time."

"Worf," sighed Kebron, "you have an absolute knack for taking all the enjoyment out of everything."

"Not true," retorted Worf. "I can see one positive aspect of this encounter."

"Oh?"

"Yes. Earlier this year, we would not have warned each other of impending danger."

Zak actually smiled at that. The Klingon was correct, of course. Their first year at the Academy had gotten off to a start even rockier than Kebron's skin. Zak's people had a long history of hatred for Klingons that had not been erased merely because the Klingons were now allies of the Federation. So Kebron had arrived at the Academy with all of his anti-Klingon prejudices solidly intact.

Worf, for his part, had spent a lifetime being raised by humans and had, many times, found himself in hostile situations merely because of who and what he was. So he had arrived at the Academy with something of a chip on his shoulder. When he and Kebron had first met, they had come to blows seconds later. The Starfleet Academy administration had chosen to solve the problem by assigning Worf and Zak to be roommates. It had seemed an idea that was at once ludicrous and, in large measure, dangerous.

In time, though, the two of them had managed to work through—if not completely work out—their differences, partly due to their prolonged exposure to each other. And partly because during another training exercise, the cadets had been convinced that their lives were genuinely threatened. It had seemed to them that the Prometheus space station, under Romulan attack, was collapsing around their ears. At that moment, when all appeared hopeless, Worf had fought to save Kebron's life even though it seemed his own end was near. The later-revealed fact that it had all been a holographic fake did not diminish Worf's bravery in Zak's eyes.

They had developed a mutual respect and even a liking for each other. They simply were loathe to admit it.

Worf and Kebron entered their quarters still arguing and stopped short in surprise.

Soleta was waiting for them.

Soleta, a Vulcan, was one of their classmates. As calm and logical as any of her people, she was at the head of the class in the field of science. This status of academic supremacy might very well be attributed to the study group that she had founded along with several other top students. Two of them were Mark McHenry, the perpetually distracted but lightning-fast astronavigational specialist, and Tania Tobias, a dedicated and determined engineering student. Worf and Zak Kebron— now a member of the study group—were vying for positions in security, but neither were absolute tops when it came to academics. Being part of the study group had helped to keep them in the upper third of their class, and when it came to combat, Worf and Zak had developed into a formidable one-two punch.

The impressive array of academic and physical talent that the group commanded had not gone unnoticed in the Academy, and they had picked up the nickname, the "Dream Team." Soleta, in particular, had seen little purpose in such nicknames, but the others in the group had warmed to it rather quickly and eventually she had taken to using it as well.

Still, Soleta rarely made such unexpected appearances without scheduling ahead. She was very precise in that regard, and tended to plan her life at least a week in advance. So Worf and Zak knew immediately that something was up.

"Soleta—?" Worf let the question dangle.

"Word just came down," she said. She rose from the chair and stepped over some of the items that had piled up on the floor. "We have a mission, off-planet."

Zak and Worf glanced at each other. The same thought was going through both their minds, but Soleta quickly put the notion to rest. "It's not another fake," she said crisply.

"Are you sure?" asked Worf warily. Once a Klingon was on his guard, he was not easily put off it. And Klingons were on their guard almost from the moment they first drew breath.

"Yes, I'm sure. We've been assigned to act as liaisons to a colony world. The circumstances are rather unique, and the Academy board felt—so I was told—

7

that, because of the unique composition of the Dream Team, we are the best suited to participate."

"I find it difficult to believe," said Zak, as skeptical as Worf, "that there's going to be something about our group—as formidable an assortment of students as we are—that would give us any sort of edge over a starship group."

"Or someone from the diplomatic corps," agreed Worf. "Or even a group of upperclassmen, if they are insistent on an Academy crew."

Soleta raised an eyebrow. "Speculation is pointless, gentlemen. We are scheduled to meet with Professor Alexander Trump at thirteen hundred hours today. Logically, we will learn at that time why we have been chosen. However, the reasoning seems fairly evident to me."

Worf and Zak looked at her blankly. "Care to illuminate us?" asked Zak.

"We have one thing that no starship, no diplomatic team, and no other group in the Academy has. Gentlemen, we have a Klingon."

And with that she walked out of their quarters, leaving the two puzzled roommates staring at each other.

"You know," said Zak after a moment, "she's right. I forgot. You are a Klingon."

"It has been brought to my attention from time to time," Worf told him gravely.

CHAPTER

Professor Alexander Trump had, in the course of his long career before coming to the Academy, traveled thousands upon thousands of light years. And it seemed like every single one was etched into his face.

Trump had occasionally been referred to—behind his back—as the Man in the Moon. This was because his face was so etched with lines and craters that it bore a resemblance to the legendary resident of that celestial body. He was not particularly old, but he carried his experience with great gravity. His hair was gray, short, and bristly. His eyes were gray and didn't seem to miss anything that happened around him. He spoke thirty languages fluently, ranging from English, Vulcan and Klingonese, to Interlak and even a bizarre form of pidgin Orion.

However, after a long and distinguished career, Trump had loudly announced that it was time for him to start taking it easier. Consequently he had accepted a teaching post at the Academy, sharing theories of xenosociety and diplomacy. He did, however, leave himself available for the occasional foray out into space. This was at his insistence. "If I don't get back out there at least once a year," he had told his superiors, "I'll lose my edge."

It was hard for anyone who had ever met Trump to believe that he could possibly lose his edge, since his flinty personality was so deeply ingrained. But he commanded enough respect that his superiors made certain to kick something his way as close to annually as they could.

Worf had never seen Trump before, for the professor stuck primarily to teaching and lecturing upperclassmen. He found himself impressed, however, by the aura of power that seemed to radiate from the man.

Trump seemed to have a perpetual squint, and now his eyes narrowed even further as he regarded Worf, Zak, Tania, Soleta and Mark, who were seated around his desk. "So," he said with a voice that sounded as leathery as his face, "you're the Dream Team. Which one of you is in charge?"

They looked at one another. It was not a question that had ever been asked of them before.

"We are all equal, sir," Worf said, after a moment.

"Course you are," said Trump, leaning back in his chair. "Some are more equal than others, however. For the purpose of this little adventure, Mr. Worf will serve as team captain, and Mr. Soleta will be the first officer. Is that acceptable to all of you?"

Soleta, Tania, and Worf nodded. McHenry, unsurprisingly, had slid off into his usual distraction, and seemed suddenly preoccupied with a particular point on the wall. Trump noticed it and looked at him questioningly, but Soleta made a gesture that seemed to say, *Don't worry about it. He's always like that.*

Zak, predictably, grunted.

"Sir, if I may, what precisely *is* the nature of this 'little adventure'?" asked Tania.

Trump sat back, steepling his fingers. "Ladies and gentlemen—you are going to be accompanying me to Dantar IV."

"Of course," said Soleta, actually sounding slightly annoyed with herself. "It was the only logical conclusion."

The others looked perplexed. "You are familiar with 'Dantar IV'?" asked Worf.

"Why am I not surprised?" said Zak. "If it's there to be known, then Soleta knows it."

"My being informed is not the surprising aspect, Mr. Kebron," Soleta told him. "What *is* surprising is that you did *not* know."

"So as to spare everyone's feelings," said Trump, who did not seem particularly impressed by the back-and-forth of the students, "I'll spell it out for you. Dantar IV is a colony world that's a Federation/Klingon co-venture. There have been previous situations with Klingons and Federation personnel on the same planet. However, in such instances, it's been a case of both groups happening to come to ground at roughly the same time, staring at each other, growling, and announcing loudly that neither of them is leaving. It's not a cooperative venture so much as an I-won't-kill-you-if-you-won't-kill-me venture.

"But Dantar IV has a different situation entirely. Dantar has been something of a test case. From the very first, it was designed to be a cooperative venture between Klingon and Federation colonization teams. Everything has been split right down the middle. Each group has an equal number of colonists, one hundred and seventy-three."

"How did they arrive at that number?" asked Tania.

"Compromise," said Trump. "In life you will generally discover that, whenever something utterly inexplicable has occurred, it's usually the result of a committee coming together and arriving at a solution that satisfies everyone and pleases no one. Dantar IV, Team, is not the most hospitable of worlds. It's hot—hot as Hades. That alone is enough to put most folks in a less-than-charitable state of mind. Combined with that is a colony world of three hundred and forty-six people who have been brought up from their earliest memories to have antipathy for the opposite race. They are laboring mightily to overcome those innate hostilities."

"And failing, I would assume," said Kebron. He glanced at Worf and said, "Believe me, I know how difficult that can be."

"I'm aware of that, Mr. Kebron," said Trump. "I read your files, both your files." He indicated Worf, and then added, "All your files, in fact. Because of the unique make-up of your particular group, it was brought to my attention that you would be the ideal squad to accompany me to Dantar. After all, Klingons in Starfleet are not exactly commonplace."

Soleta looked triumphantly—although her natural reserve reined that in—at Worf and Zak. But Worf was frowning even more than he usually did. "I cannot say, sir, that I am particularly pleased about this."

This drew surprised looks from the others. "Is that a fact, Mr. Worf?" said Trump quietly.

"I do not think that race should factor into the choice of mission personnel," Worf said. "Ability and experience should be the sole criteria."

"I see." Trump considered this for a moment. "That is a very noble and honorable attitude to have, Mr. Worf." And then he added, "It's also stupid as sin."

"Sir—?"

"The galaxy is a harsh place, Mr. Worf. We've made strides, heaven knows. Tremendous strides. But it's still full of strife and hostility. We have an obligation to use every trick, every stunt, every advantage that we can possibly muster in our dealings with it. If it's academic superiority, then we use that. If it's quickness of wits, quickness of hands, quickness of thought, we make use of that, too. And if it happens that the circumstances of your birth are going to be of benefit, then we use that as well. It's a tool, Mr. Worf. Starfleet is a tool. Starships are tools. And your being a Klingon is a tool as well, no different from any of the others. The only difference is that you've decided to be oversensitive about it. I suggest you dispense with that state of mind immediately. It will not be of benefit to you at all. If

you want to survive in space, Mr. Worf—and all of you, for that matter—then you would be well advised to use everything you've got going for you, up to and including the pattern of your DNA structure. Because you're going to need everything and more. Are we clear on this?''

"Yes, sir," said Worf. There were nods from all around.

"Good. Now," he leaned back, interlacing his fingers once more, "we will be performing a variety of functions once we get to Dantar IV. We'll be checking over various procedures to make certain that they're running properly. We will be," and he smiled slightly, "the voice of reason, hopefully settling any hostilities and unresolved disputes that might have arisen during the past months. You see, the dispatches we've been receiving from the colony heads—dispatches that the Klingon Empire have been receiving as well, I might add—have made it very clear that they are having trouble keeping the peace."

"Have they requested arbitration?"

Trump snickered. "Please, Mister Soleta. Colonists are far too proud to ask for help, although they will not shun it if offered. What *has* been said in the most recent dispatch is," and he glanced at his computer screen, " 'Hostilities so widespread that it seems impossible for any except outside arbitrators to settle them.' That is the closest they'd come to requesting help. It is, however, quite clear to the Federation. It is also quite likely clear to the Klingons, although how they will react is anyone's guess." He leaned back in his chair. "In short, Team, you will be offering needed help in the variety of fields that you represent."

"Sir, as accomplished as we might be in those fields," Tania pointed out, "certainly there are members of Starfleet who have far more experience."

Trump looked incredulous. "You know, either you are the most modest bunch of cadets I've ever seen, or else the most phenomenally suspicious." His eyes narrowed. "Ohhhh—of course. Of course you're suspicious. You're looking for the catch. You think this might be another Prometheus test run."

They shifted uncomfortably in their seats. "It had crossed our minds," admitted Zak.

The professor shook his head. "You know, I've been at odds with the Academy curriculum board over that sort of stunt for years now. On the one hand they want to keep you on your toes; on the other they want to watch out for your safety, particularly at the beginning. So they come up with stunts like that space station under attack holoscenario. I suppose I can't blame you, Team, for your suspicions. All I can tell you is this: This isn't a trick. This isn't a test. This is the real thing. This is the type of thing you've been training for. With all deference to Mr. Worf's concerns, I openly admit it: He's right. The combination of your collective academic success and his ancestry has put you in the prime spot to act as my backup and diplomatic team. And to be honest, the fact that you're *not* full Starfleet is also something of an advantage. As distrustful as the Federation colonists might be of the Klingons and vice versa, they share a collective antipathy for Starfleet as well.

Call it a holdover from centuries ago when organizations similar to Starfleet were military in nature and viewed everything in terms of, 'Now, how can we turn this into a weapon so we can add another means of wiping the human race off the face of the Earth?' " He shook his head. "So much suspicion—and worse, so many understandable reasons for it. It is a problem, definitely."

And then his voice turned hard. "The question, people, is—are you going to be part of the problem, or part of the solution?"

The first officer looked at the captain. The captain nodded.

"When do we leave, sir?" asked Soleta.

CHAPTER

The Starship *Repulse* sailed through the ether of space.

Worf sat in the Forward Lounge, looking out at the stars as they sailed past, pinpoint streaks of light. It was a remarkable sensation, being on a vessel that cut through the vacuum as easily as a sharpened knife could slit the throat of an enemy. . . .

He shook his head. Here he was, eyeing a future in Starfleet, and he was using metaphors that centered on destruction and death. Clearly, he thought, becoming a true Starfleet officer involved far more than academics. It required a complete reordering of one's thought process.

That day in Trump's office, as recent as it had been, now seemed a very distant memory. Any lingering doubts about the veracity of their new assignment had evaporated when they'd transferred from the long-distance shuttle to the transporter room of the *Repulse*.

Tania had confided to Worf that she had had the fanciful belief that she could actually feel the pulse of the mighty starship's engines beneath her feet as she walked the decks.

He hadn't seen much of Tania since they boarded the ship. For that matter, he hadn't seen much of any of his friends. They had been wandering the ship, exploring her from stem to stern. At most there had been quick waves in the corridors or an occasional meal together.

It gave Worf pause as he considered the future of the Dream Team. Worf came to the surprising realization that, whenever he imagined his future in Starfleet, he started picturing himself aboard a vessel with all the members of his study group alongside him. Tania down in engineering, Soleta as science officer, himself and Zak running security, Mac navigating the ship.

Well, that last one actually gave Worf a touch of nervousness. Despite all the time that he had gotten to know Mark "Mac" McHenry and his amazing capabilities, the youth still made him nervous.

Mac was the only other member of the Dream Team present in the Forward Lounge at that moment. He was not, however, sitting with Worf. He was over in a table by the corner, surrounded by four *Repulse* crewmen. They were holding playing cards, and one of them, Worf could hear, was explaining to Mac the intricacies of playing poker. Mac, for once, was not in his usual semidream state of consciousness. He seemed totally focused, nodding and clearly taking in everything the senior officer was telling him. The other officers were smiling and nudging each other.

Worf shook his head. "Fools," he muttered.

"Who's a fool?" a voice asked behind him.

Worf turned and saw the smiling face of the ship's commanding officer. Immediately Worf was on his feet.

"Captain Taggert," Worf rumbled with a deferential nod of his head.

"Please, please, Mister—Worf, is it?" Worf nodded, and Taggert continued, "Take your seat. Do you mind if I join you?"

"I would be honored!"

Taggert nodded and sat down opposite him. He had a pleasant, thoughtful look on his face. His hair was just starting to gray, but he had a salt-and-pepper beard that was clearly way in advance of the hair on his head when it came to silvering up. "So—" and he indicated the poker players, "it would seem that your classmate over there has fallen in with a bad crowd."

"Sir—?" Worf looked over toward the card players, trying to imagine which of these officers might be some sort of villain.

"They sense a pigeon, Mr. Worf," said Taggert. "Your Mr. McHenry seems—how shall I put it?"

"Incompetent?" offered Worf.

"I doubt I would have put it quite that bluntly, but admittedly, yes. He does seem one of the odder cadets to trod the decks of the *Repulse*."

Worf looked back at the card players. Mac wasn't even looking at his cards. He was holding up a chip and studying with intense interest the manner in which the light reflected off it.

"Odd, yes," admitted Worf. "And he appears incompetent, I know. However, Captain, Mr. McHenry will win the game."

"You're joking. Mr. Worf, believe me, I value my officers highly, but I have no illusions as far as their mercy on an inexperienced card player goes. Those sharks will eat him alive."

"With all due respect, sir, you are wrong," said Worf simply.

Taggert shrugged. "We'll see."

They were silent for a moment. "So what do you think of the *Repulse,* Mr. Worf?"

"She is the most magnificent vessel I have ever seen," Worf said flatly. "She does you honor. My father spoke often of such ships, but his descriptions did little to convey her full impact."

"She is a beauty," Taggert said with satisfaction. "Newly commissioned. I'm her first captain. It's an incredible feeling; like so many when it comes to Starfleet and space exploration, a feeling that no words can adequately describe. And she has a fine crew."

"Yes, sir."

Worf's terse response prompted a raised eyebrow from Taggert. "You do not endorse that statement?"

"They seem—quite competent and knowledgeable in their duties."

"But—?"

Worf looked down at his drink, staring at his own reflection. "Permission to speak freely, sir?"

"Interesting." Taggert smiled. "Most cadets I've encountered smile and nod and say whatever they think the captain wants to hear. And here you have something you want to say that you feel is so compelling that you want to make sure you won't be charged with insubordination."

Worf was silent.

"Very well, Mr. Worf. Say what's on your mind. Has someone on my crew given you difficulties?"

"No, sir," said Worf, gazing downward once more. "However, I get a distinct sense of—unease—from the ship's personnel whenever I am around. Many times I see people perform—what is the expression?—a 'double-take.' They see a Klingon, and then they see the uniform, and they have to look again because they have difficulty reconciling the two."

"And you find that annoying?"

Worf sighed. "I find it disappointing. When I first came to the Academy, I experienced hostility on the part of numerous classmates. I had thought that Starfleet officers would react differently, that is all."

Taggert frowned. "Has anyone been rude to you? Said you were not fit to wear the uniform of an Academy trainee?"

"No, sir."

"They've just looked surprised to see you."

"Yes, sir."

Taggert laughed. Worf was slightly startled at the captain's reaction.

"Mr. Worf, you had me worried there for a moment."

"Sir—?"

"Tell me, Mr. Worf, if you saw a troop of Klingon warriors heading your way—dressed in silver and black leather, bristling and bearded and as fierce as Klingon warriors can be—and one of their number was a blond haired, fair-skinned human, what would your reaction be? I mean, think of it: a human being, dressed as a Klingon, speaking perfect Klingonese but a head shorter and about a hundred pounds lighter than any of his associates."

"It would seem—odd," admitted Worf.

"To put it mildly," agreed Taggert. "Don't be any less surprised when the crew does double-takes whenever a tall, young Klingon strides down the corridor dressed as a cadet. It is, quite simply, an uncommon sight. Going through Starfleet training doesn't rob you of your ability to be surprised. What it *does* do is force you to take those surprises on their own terms. Understand?''

Worf nodded, beginning to.

''Now if anyone says or does anything to make you feel *unwelcome*—well, that's a different story. That is behavior that simply will not be tolerated in a Starfleet officer. Beyond that, though—well, you might as well get used to the fact that, as the first Klingon to enter Starfleet, you're going to turn a lot of heads. And you know what? Let 'em stare. Getting noticed can be a valuable tool for advancement. If people are watching you already, and then you perform at or above expectations, that can only bode well for you. Right?''

''Yes, sir. I—suppose you are right.''

''Of course I'm right,'' said Taggert. ''I'm the captain.'' He sighed, looking out at the stars. ''You know, Mr. Worf, I'm relieved that this destructive conflict between the Klingon Empire and the Federation has finally ended. It was a long road from the Khitomer Conference to the circumstances that brought about your sitting here in the *Repulse* Forward Lounge.''

''Why are you 'relieved,' sir?''

''Because the galaxy is a tricky enough place to navigate, and the Klingons are one of the most formidable peoples I've ever encountered. I have a daughter, Mr. Worf. Her name is Ariel. She's in Starfleet, too. Loved what her old man did and decided to follow in his footsteps. My fantasy is that she winds up taking over the command of the *Repulse* when I'm ready to move on.''

"It is possible, sir," said Worf.

"Yes, it is. Not likely, of course. But possible. And being a father, naturally I want things to be as safe as possible for her, even though deep space is one of the less safe places in which a person can go running about. And if she's commanding a starship in a galaxy where the Klingons are with us, rather than against us, well, that's one less thing for me to worry about. Understand?"

"Yes, Captain. Completely."

An astonished gasp and a series of moans reached their ears. Worf and Taggert turned and looked at the source: the card game.

Mac had just shown his hand, to the dismay and irritation of the older, more experienced card players. They threw down their cards in disgust as Mac pulled the chips in the pot over to him. The stack in front of him had grown to huge proportions.

One of the crewmen was moaning, "I don't believe it. I bet my tricorder that he couldn't beat my hand! I love that tricorder; it's got all the latest features!"

"Good," said Mac calmly. "I could use one."

Taggert was gaping in surprise, and he looked back to Worf. "Mr. Worf, I stand corrected," he said. "Your Mr. McHenry is taking the *Repulse* ace poker crew to the cleaners."

"We call him the 'Quiet Killer,' " Worf told him, which was something of an exaggeration. Actually they usually called him "Airhead," although Tania insisted it was meant affectionately.

"Perhaps you should join in, Mr. Worf. Imagine if a

second cadet came in and raked them over the coals as well."

"I see little point in card games, sir," said Worf stiffly. "Games should be the type that test a warrior's ability to survive, not a trivial exercise in gambling."

"Don't sell poker short, Mr. Worf. Learning when to bluff, when to gamble, when to hold tight to your cards, and when to fold up and go home—those are lessons that—"

Taggert's communicator beeped. He tapped it and said, "Taggert here."

"Captain, this is Woods. We're approaching Dantar IV, but sensors have just detected another ship."

"Identified?"

"Yes sir. It's a Klingon ship, sir."

Taggert and Worf exchanged looks, and Taggert was immediately on his feet. "I'll be right up, Mr. Woods. Taggert out."

Taggert started toward the door, and then stopped and turned to Worf. "Have you ever been up on the bridge of a starship, Mr. Worf?"

Worf could do nothing to keep the surprise out of his face. "Sir—is this because we may be encountering a Klingon ship?"

"Of course it is. There may be an alliance, Mr. Worf, but it's not such an old, familiar one that we toss caution to the wind. Besides—" and he smiled—"this will be a chance to see if only Starfleet personnel do double-takes when they see a Klingon in a Starfleet uniform, or whether it's a trait they share with Klingons."

CHAPTER

The Klingon battle cruiser filled the viewscreen of the *Repulse.*

Worf stood above and to the right of Captain Taggert, who was settling into his command chair. Worf had seen the bridge before when the cadets had been given a tour. Everything was neatly ordered, with calm, muted colors that set a relaxed mood. Relaxed, yet with an undercurrent of efficiency. The command chair was situated dead center. To the captain's immediate right was the chair for first officer Greer, a strapping young man who was the second in command. The conn and ops stations were forward. There was a raised upper deck that had such stations as engineering and tactical where Worf was now standing, facing the viewscreen.

The Klingon ship looked as if it were staring straight at them. Right down their throats.

Worf felt a swell of pride and excitement. His memories of an actual Klingon vessel were so distant and vague as to be useless. And now, here one was. With graceful, curving lines, it seemed as if all the strength and majesty of the Klingon Empire were summed up in this one powerful package.

For the briefest of moments Worf imagined himself standing, not on the bridge of a starship, but on the bridge of a Klingon vessel. What would he be like, he wondered, if he were side-by-side with Klingon warriors, contemplating the image of a Starfleet ship on a viewer? Would he be regarding with contempt a people that he barely knew, because of his own notions about the types of individuals that populated a typical Starfleet vessel—the same individuals who were now his compatriots, his co-workers. If he were part of the Klingon Empire, he might very well be confident in the superiority of all things Klingon and the inferiority of all things non-Klingon.

"We're receiving an incoming transmission from the Klingon vessel," said Lieutenant Topper from ops.

"Put them on," said Taggert, crossing his legs. Worf was fascinated to see that Taggert appeared to be putting on an air of total confidence. Being a tough, calm, Starfleet officer was the role he was assuming, applying his "command face" to deal with whatever difficulties presented themselves.

The screen flickered for just a moment, and then the scowling face of a Klingon appeared.

The bridge of the Klingon vessel was barely visible behind him. In contrast to the *Repulse* bridge, the Klingon bridge was dark and foreboding. What little illumination there was lit the Klingon faces in mysterious fashion. The control chair for the Klingon commander was also dead center, but hanging from a support strut in the ceiling. Dim green, red, and yellow lights flickered all around, the only spots of color in an environment that was mostly gray and black. Worf stared at the commander with rapt attention. It was the first Klingon he'd seen since he was a child, and he felt a thrill go through him. Despite all the care and love his human parents had given him, he had still never been fully able to shake a feeling of loneliness and isolation. In a universe surrounded by humans, the knowledge that there were others of his kind out there was very little comfort. Especially when a young Worf was having difficulty finding anyone his own age who shared his temperament or outlook on life.

"This is Captain Kora of the Klingon cruiser *K'leela*," said the Klingon. "I am . . ."

Then he stopped. His eyes widened in astonishment. Worf knew that Klingons rarely allowed themselves to be caught off guard.

He was gazing straight at Worf.

Taggert was aware of this, of course, but was utterly calm about it. "Yes, Captain?" he asked.

"Who is that?" Captain Kora was close to losing his composure.

"Who is who?"

"You have a Klingon on board your ship! I do not believe it!"

Worf would have felt tremendously unsettled at that moment, if it weren't for Taggert's dry-as-dust handling

of the situation. "I don't quite understand, Captain," he said. "You have lots of Klingons on your ship. I have no difficulty believing that. We have only one Klingon. That seems far less of a stretch."

"Who are you?" The question was directed at Worf.

Worf opened his mouth to speak, but remembered to look to Taggert for permission first. It would have been a serious breach of protocol to start talking with the commander of another vessel while one's captain was present. Taggert gave the matter a moment's thought, and then nodded. "I am Worf," he said, moving down to stand beside Captain Taggert.

"Worf? You are Worf? And beyond that, who are you?"

"Worf, son of Mogh."

"Beyond that, he is a Starfleet cadet, and as such, my concern," said Taggert, clearly deciding that the discussion had gone far enough. "Likewise, are you, Captain Kora. You have approached us, hailed us, all without knowing that a Klingon was standing on this bridge. I presume that you had something to say. I would suggest then, sir, that you tell me what that might be, so we can proceed from there."

Kora, with effort, forced his attention back to Taggert. "I wish to know if you are en route to Dantar IV."

"Yes."

"Why?"

"Ah, ah," said Taggert, raising a scolding finger. "There is no rule in Starfleet, Captain Kora, that says

I have to respond to any and all questions. You asked me where we were going, and I answered. Now I ask you a question: Why do you wish to know?''

Kora frowned, clearly considering several comebacks before deciding that the best response was to be straightforward. "We are also en route to Dantar," admitted Kora. "We understand that there has been some hostility between the colonists, and we are sending a team to oversee conditions there and settle any disputes."

"Settle how?" asked Taggert.

"Fairly. I presume that the Federation has no objection to matters being handled in such a manner."

"None whatsoever. Just as I presume that you have no problem with the fact that we are likewise sending our own team."

"Ahhh," Kora said, understanding dawning. "With Worf to serve as the token Klingon presence to convey the Federation's 'sincerity.' ''

"With Mr. Worf," corrected Taggert, "to serve in his capacity as a Starfleet cadet. Nothing more than that, Captain."

"And is Worf to serve as head of your expedition?"

"No, that is being left to a senior ambassador: Alexander Trump."

There was clear recognition on Kora's face. "Trump. I know of him. A good man," Kora said almost grudgingly.

"I will tell him you think so."

"Very well, then, Captain," said Kora after a moment. "There is no reason that matters cannot proceed.

In the Dantar IV issue, we can assume that a fair settlement is in the best interests of both the Klingons and the Federation. Would you say?"

"I'd have no need to say it," Taggert replied, "since you have already said it so well."

Kora nodded slightly, but as his image blinked out, he cast one last look toward Worf. It made the young Klingon feel very uncomfortable.

The Klingon battle cruiser angled away, and moments later the sleek warship was matching the speed and course of the *Repulse* exactly.

"Your opinion, Mr. Worf."

"Sir?"

Taggert had turned in his chair and was facing the cadet. "Your opinion of the situation. Is it your impression that Captain Kora is going to act in a reasonable manner?"

"It is my impression that Captain Kora will act like a Klingon," Worf said. "No more, or less, than that. The Klingon team will have its instructions, as we have ours. I am certain that each will act in the appropriate way."

"That's good to hear, Mr. Worf," said Taggert. "That's very good to hear."

CHAPTER

The first thing the cadets noticed upon beaming down to the surface of Dantar was that the place seemed absolutely deserted. Even though they knew they were beaming to the outskirts of town, it hadn't quite prepared them for the sense of utter desolation. It was an eerie feeling.

This was quickly obscured, however, by the second thing to hit the cadets—the heat which seemed to roll off the ground. The transporter effect had barely finished when some of them—most notably Tania and Mark—staggered slightly. It was an abrupt change, shifting from the comfortable environment of a starship to the grueling surface of Dantar IV.

The cadets and Trump carried supply sacks on their backs. Such was necessary since the starship, along with the Klingon vessel, had left orbit. For the ships to stay on station until the mission was completed was not possible, because they were not sure how long matters were going to take. Might be a week, might be two.

In any event, colony world supplies were always at a premium, and the last thing the group wanted to be was any sort of burden on the colonists. The arid world of Dantar IV was burdensome enough for its residents.

The landing party also had visors to protect them against the heat of the atmosphere and the glare of the sun. The visors were tinted and had promptly gone to maximum darkness the moment the group had arrived on the planet surface. It helped significantly, although not completely. The sun was still the brightest that most of them had ever experienced.

Worf felt the assault of the surroundings, but he was too stubborn to give any indication that it affected him. Zak, with his tough and durable hide, seemed indifferent to it.

Soleta, for her part, took in deep lungfuls of air, to Tania's amazement. "What's with you?" Tania gasped, feeling her own throat closing up.

"It feels like home," Soleta replied. "Thin air, and hot. Yes, it's very much like Vulcan."

"Terrific," muttered Tania.

Alexander Trump didn't seem particularly perturbed. Then again, his determined expression seemed permanently attached to his face. Unchanging, unwavering, inflexible. He surveyed the terrain as a hunter would.

The transporter arrival site was at the outskirts of the town.

Town might have been too strong a word.

Most of the buildings were no taller than two stories.

They were prefabricated constructions, designed for utility and function rather than form. So the town (for lack of a better term) was not one of the more attractive places in which one was likely to find oneself.

The buildings were all the same color—white. The reason was simple. White was inherently a cooler color, since it reflected sunlight, as opposed to darker colors, such as black, which absorbed it. On a colony world such as Dantar IV, everything was at a premium—food, supplies, energy sources. Everything was thought of either in terms of what the colonists had brought with them, or what they were able to derive from the planet itself. In this case it was energy efficient to use white.

Of course there were supply ships that came through. But the entire point of a colony world was to make a place that was self-sufficient. One could not base one's entire life on waiting for the next shipload of supplies. Colonists had a large measure of pride when it came to accomplishing what they set out to do.

As a result, there was a love/hate relationship between colony worlds and their sponsors. On the one hand colonists needed, and appreciated, the support that was provided by organizations such as the Federation. On the other hand creating and maintaining a colony took a certain degree of determination and independence; consequently, the colonists resented having to depend on anyone but themselves.

A breeze started to kick up. Dirt began to swirl around on the ground like miniature cyclones, and Tania sighed in relief. "At last, some cool air."

"You've been here thirty seconds," said Trump. "I wouldn't let myself get rattled so easily by the heat if I were you."

"Where is everyone?" asked Worf.

"I'm not sure. Maybe it's too hot to be out. Maybe they're planning to jump out and yell 'Surprise.' "

At that moment, the door to one the buildings at the far end of the compound slid open. A man stood in the doorway waving to them and shouting, but he was too far away for them to make out what he was saying.

At least, most of them couldn't make out what he was saying.

Soleta, for her part, with her formidable Vulcan ears, heard him clearly. "A storm," she said. "He's saying something about a storm coming up. . . ."

As if on cue, the wind which Tania had found so comforting now began to show its fierce side. It kicked up furiously, sending pebbles and rocks skidding across the hard ground. Sand started to blow around, and if it weren't for the visors they were wearing, they'd all have been blinded within moments.

"Come on!" shouted Trump. None of them needed further urging, and they bolted across the compound toward the building.

Worf dropped toward the back of the group, automatically bringing up the rear to make sure that everyone got to safety. It was fortunate that he did, for the tip of Tania's boot hit a small fissure in the ground as she ran. She emitted a little shriek and pitched forward. Worf grabbed her from behind, catching her before she struck the ground. She staggered, nodding that she was all right. Soleta slowed, and between the two of them, they helped Tania limp the rest of the way.

They approached the shelter and, through the swirling sand, Worf was able to see Trump standing in the doorway, gesturing for them to hurry. Moments later everyone was within the confines of the simple but functional shelter.

"You all right, Tobias?" asked Trump.

"Just hurt my ankle. I'll be fine." But she winced as she lowered herself into a chair. "Thanks Soleta, Worf."

Worf grunted acknowledgement. To him, thanks were unnecessary. Taking care of one's teammates was, quite simply, something that was expected. He literally could do no less.

He stood up and lifted his goggles, which made it a bit easier to see.

The room was fairly cramped, crowded with electronics equipment that didn't look to be state of the art. Much of it appeared held together with spit and bailing wire. There were two desks in opposite corners of the room. One was somewhat disorganized, covered with various reference materials and displaying a general air of barely controlled chaos. The other desk was spotless.

A door led off into another room, but it was closed. Trump and the cadets were the only ones in the main room at present.

Through the door they could hear voices, and Worf felt a flash of recognition. Some of the words being spoken were unmistakably Klingonese. They were alternating with English. Clearly a conversation was being held on several levels: There were Klingons talking with one another in their natural tongue, while Terrans were discoursing with one another as well. And then, every so often, everyone would be speaking English, obviously for the purpose of joint communication. Klingons generally found it easier to converse in English than to wait for Terrans to use the hand-held universal translator.

"What are they saying, Worf?" asked Soleta. "The Klingons, I mean."

Worf drew himself up, looking surprised. "You wish for me to eavesdrop?"

"They are saying," Alexander Trump told them calmly, "that handling the Federation people will not be difficult. That Starfleet personnel remain intimidated by Klingons, and showing them who is in a superior position of authority will be easily accomplished. They're saying they can keep us in line and give Klingon interests maximum priority."

Worf looked at Trump in surprise. He'd heard about Trump's ease with language, but it was something else again to see it displayed so openly.

Several human voices were heard demanding that the Klingons talk to *them,* blast it, not to each other. This prompted another major discussion, with voices even louder.

"Perhaps we should go in and—"

"And what, Mr. Worf? Lay down the law? Show them who's in charge?" The edges of his mouth turned up ever so slightly, which was about as close to a smile as he usually came. "I don't think so. That would play right into the preconception they have of us. No, Mr. Worf, we wait. We wait for them to come to us, and then we are conciliatory and patient and thoughtful. Our job here is to guide, not to push. Understood?"

"Yes, sir," said Worf, who was not one hundred percent sure. Pushing was a simpler solution, one that he strongly supported.

Tania cleared her throat. "Excuse me, but my ankle is killing me. Is there any chance that someone . . . ?"

Mark McHenry walked over to her, pulling his pack off and rummaging around in it. Tania eyed him suspiciously. "Do you know what you're doing?" she asked.

"Of course," he replied calmly. After a few moments, he pulled out a small cylindrical object and activated it. It made a soft humming noise, and he passed it over her ankle.

She looked genuinely surprised. "That feels a lot better," she acknowledged. "Thanks, Mac. What is that thing? How does it work?"

"I have no idea," he replied cheerfully.

"You said you knew what you were doing!"

"I did know what I was doing. I was going through my backpack. But as for what this thing is"—and he shrugged—"your guess is as good as mine."

She rolled her eyes. "Mac, you're hopeless."

"I hope so."

The door opened, and a haggard but determined man with curly black hair came out, extending his hand to Trump. "Hello there. Paul Dini, Federation administrator. I apologize for the weather."

"You made the weather? Great. Do you use machinery or do you just, you know, wave a large stick?" asked Mac.

Dini gave Mark McHenry an odd look, and Trump very quickly stepped in. He introduced everyone in the Dream Team, and then continued, "We didn't mean to eavesdrop, but it sounded from out here as if you were having a few problems."

Dini sighed loudly. "I wouldn't say that. To be specific, I don't think the words 'a few' begin to cover it."

"Where's your co-administrator?"

"Khard is still in the next room, talking to the Klingon envoys. These other Klingons just showed up, minutes before you people did . . ." His voice altered into one of deep concern. "Were you expecting this? Did you know the Klingons were going to send their own people?"

"Not until we reached this system," replied Trump.

"Yes, well—I suppose it was a bit late then." He sighed once more. "It has not been easy. In this kind of situation, the slightest look, the mischosen word, can lead to all manner of anger and mistrust. This is supposed to be a cooperative venture, not an uncooperative one."

"Don't concern yourself, Mr. Dini," said Trump.

"My crack backup team is on the job. So why don't you bring out the other Klingons and we can try to get things sorted out."

Dini took a moment to study Worf, and then he chucked a thumb at him while looking at Trump. "He's on our side?"

Worf was about to bite off an indignant answer, but Trump replied instead. "I suspect, Mr. Dini, that that is the problem here. There are no 'sides' here. It should not be you versus them. There should just be 'us.'"

"Uh huh," said Dini, not looking particularly convinced. He turned and walked into the next room, and moments later the Klingons were filing out.

In the lead was Khard. He was not wearing the traditional Klingon uniform, but even his civilian clothes had a severe and military caste to them. And he was followed by three young Klingons, two male and one—female.

Worf was vaguely startled, as if a switch had gone off in his head. He had only the most remote memories of young females who had been his playmates (if such a word could be applied to the activities of juvenile Klingons) when he was growing up on Khitomer. And since that time he'd had no interaction with any other Klingons at all, much less females.

He found himself staring at the female. She appeared to be about his age. Her hair was long and thick, and her eyes seemed to be blazing with inner fire. She was scowling. And then Worf realized that, in particular, she was scowling at him.

Worf drew himself up, breaking eye contact with her

as he looked over toward Trump. He felt that it was very necessary that he take his cues from the experienced professor. And besides, for some reason, he suddenly felt uncomfortable about the way the female Klingon was looking at him.

"Alexander Trump," said Dini formally, "this is Khard, the leader of the Klingon colonists."

Khard stepped forward and extended a hand. Trump looked at it in surprise for a moment before shaking it firmly. "You shake hands, sir?" said Trump.

"I have tried to make allowances for human customs," rumbled Khard. He glanced significantly at Dini. "It has not always been easy."

"If it were easy," said Trump, "then what possible challenge would that be for a Klingon?"

Khard grunted acknowledgment of the statement. He stepped back, and Dini introduced the other three young Klingons as warriors-in-training. Pointing from left to right, he said, "And newly arrived from the Klingon Empire to perform essentially the same function that you're here to do, Mr. Trump: Gowr—"

The one called Gowr nodded slightly. He was the shortest of the three, although that was still enough to make him taller than the average Terran. He was also extremely broad shouldered, so much so that it seemed as if he would most likely have difficulty fitting through a door comfortably.

"Kodash," continued Dini.

Kodash, by contrast, was the tallest, and although all three of them looked rather fierce, he was definitely the most intense. He had a fairly long moustache, with small metal caps at the ends.

He seemed to be staring at Zak Kebron, and Zak was doing nothing to indicate that he was thrilled to be looking at Kodash. Worf realized that he might have to be ready to deal with a variety of problems, because although Zak had had time to get used to being around Worf, he was still fighting many ingrained prejudices toward Klingons in general. Add into the mix that many Klingons had no great love for the Brikar, and one was forced to come to the conclusion that the mix could be a very volatile one indeed.

Then Dini indicated the female Klingon, and Worf's attention was drawn to her once more. She, for her part, was making no effort to hide the fact that she was staring openly at Worf.

"And this," said Dini, "is—" And then he hesitated. "I'm sorry, what was it again?"

"K'Ehleyr," she said brusquely.

"K'Ehleyr. Thank you. I apologize; I'm not always the best when it comes to names. My esteemed Klingon associates, these are the representatives from the Federation: Alexander Trump, noted diplomat, scholar on xenosociety, and two-time winner of the Zee Magnes prize. With him is a special team from Starfleet Academy, consisting of Tania Tobias, engineering specialist; Mark McHenry, astronav specialist—"

"I can play cards," said McHenry, looking rather pleased with himself.

Dini looked at him uncertainly once more, and then continued, "Soleta, science specialist; Zak Kebron, security specialist; and, likewise security specialist, Worf."

The Klingons were regarding Worf with what seemed a mixture of curiosity and contempt. "Worf, is it?" asked K'Ehleyr.

"That is correct," he said. "Worf, son of Mogh."

"How—curious."

Nothing was said for a long moment, and then Trump clapped his hands.

"I think," he said, "that perhaps we should get down to work."

"Yes,"said Dini quickly. "I couldn't agree more." He glanced at an indicator on the wall and nodded approvingly. "The winds are dying down. That's a relief. When we have one of our occasional sandstorms kicking up, there's really nothing much that we can do except wait for it to settle down. But it seems to be subsiding, so we can all be thankful for that."

Except that the way Zak was looking at the Klingons, and the way the Klingons were looking at Zak—and, for that matter, Worf—Worf had the uneasy feeling that other, more serious storms, were waiting just beyond the horizon. And those storms were going to be originating from somewhere other than the atmosphere.

CHAPTER

"Why didn't they shake hands?"

The Dream Team was in the visitor's barracks that had been set up for them. To say accommodations were spare would have been generous. Metal bunks lined the walls, and the main source of light was the windows. Nevertheless, the cadets adapted to the situation with a certain degree of resignation.

Tania walked about gingerly, but gained confidence with every step, as the others stowed their gear. At one point, though, she stopped, leaned against a bedpost, and addressed the question about shaking hands to Trump.

Trump smiled and said, "I'll let Mr. Worf tell you."

She turned and looked questioningly at Worf. Worf was mildly surprised that Trump had kicked the query over to him, but he mentally shrugged.

"It relates to the origins of the Terran handshake,"

he said. "When one would greet an opponent, open hands were extended and grasped. The reason was to show that no one present had a weapon on them. Klingons, however, are always expected to have weapons on them at all times. To imply that you think a Klingon is unarmed would be the highest insult."

"But Worf, you're not armed," said Tania.

"She has you there, Worf," Zak agreed. "It's specifically against Starfleet rules for cadets to carry any weapons on them."

"Yes, it is," said Worf. "That is an unfortunate regulation, in my opinion."

Tania dropped down onto her bunk and pushed at the mattress. She shook her head. "It's like a rock. Anyone have a better mattress?"

"They're all the same," said Soleta. "You will survive."

Tania turned to Worf. "What did you think of the Klingon emissaries, Worf?"

"Why ask me?"

"I think that's fairly obvious."

Soleta said thoughtfully, "The Klingon female seemed rather interested in you, Worf."

"Nonsense."

The door opened and the three Klingons entered slowly. They stopped and regarded the Federation crew for a moment in silence before striding over to a partitioned area that had been set up at the far corner of the room.

"Note how they hide themselves," Zak commented.

"It is not a matter of hiding," Worf said. "Klingons do not leave themselves exposed to ambush."

"You mean they're concerned that someone might kick open the door and start shooting?" asked Tania.

"It never hurts to anticipate all possibilities," Worf said.

"Notice," said Soleta drily, "that if someone did burst in and launch an attack, we would now wind up being the targets."

That comment did not draw any enthusiastic response.

On the other side of the partition and out of earshot, the three Klingons unpacked their few belongings. K'Ehleyr was seated on the edge of her bunk. She punched the mattress in annoyance and shook her head disgustedly. Gowr glanced over at her. "What is the problem?" he asked.

"They call this a firm mattress?" She picked it up and tossed it off the bed, a solid, unadorned slab of metal which K'Ehleyr now thumped. It made a hollow sound and she nodded. "Much better."

Kodash turned to face his compatriots. "I do not know which I have a more difficult time believing from that Federation crew: the Brikar or the Klingon."

"Keep your voice down," K'Ehleyr said.

"Why?"

"Because I said so," she said firmly.

He glowered at her for a moment, and then in a lowered voice he said, "Those obnoxious Brikar. The most insufferable race in the galaxy, aside from the Kreel.

And as if that is not enough, that . . ." Words seemed to fail him in describing Worf. "What would you call him? Is he truly one of us? A Klingon? Could there be some sort of mistake?"

"A Klingon he may be," said Gowr. "But one of us? Hardly."

Kodash looked thoughtful for a moment. "But what is he *doing* there with them? Is he there voluntarily? Maybe they're holding him prisoner, or perhaps he has been brainwashed."

Shaking her head, K'Ehleyr said, "I don't think so. I'm not certain what his situation is."

"Then you have to find out," Kodash said.

She sniffed. "Me? Why me?"

"Because he could not take his eyes off you."

"Oh, don't be ridiculous," she replied.

"Think about it, K'Ehleyr," Gowr said. "This Worf—he is one of two things. Either he is a traitor and deserter from the Empire, which, judging by his youth, I somehow doubt. Or else, as insane as this may sound, he may have been raised by humans."

"Raised by *humans?* What sort of Klingon is raised by humans?"

"That, K'Ehleyr, is what we want to find out. And you—"

"Forget it."

"You are just the Klingon to find out," Gowr continued firmly. "Am I right, Kodash?"

"You are absolutely right, Gowr."

"You are both out of your limited minds," she informed them. "I do not like him. He most certainly does not like me. I am here to do my job, and I suggest that the both of you do yours. Clear?"

"But—"

"Clear?"

"Clear," said Gowr. Kodash nodded assent.

K'Ehleyr flopped back on the hard surface, her fingers interlaced behind her head. Gowr and Kodash moved away from her, and looked at one another significantly.

And Gowr mouthed, "She will do it."

To which Kodash replied silently, "I know."

Meantime, K'Ehleyr could not get the image of Worf out of her mind. She had met him only briefly, and yet somehow she had the impression that he was different from any Klingon she had ever met.

The thing was, she wasn't entirely sure whether that was good or bad.

CHAPTER

The Terran colonist, whose name was Cannelli, seemed ready to haul off and slug the Klingon colonist, whose name was Korm. "You're doing it deliberately!"

"Of course I am doing it deliberately!" snapped back Korm. "I enjoy it!"

"You hear? You hear?" shouted Cannelli.

Seated facing the two disputing parties were Trump, Worf, K'Ehleyr, Dini, and Khard. "Yes, Mr. Cannelli, we hear," said Trump patiently.

"This has been going on for weeks!"

"Do you think I have enjoyed it?" said Korm. "Do you think these weeks of your complaining has been a pleasant experience? How am I supposed to live my life?"

"How am I supposed to get any sleep?"

"Gentlemen, gentlemen," said Trump, raising a hand. "Certainly some sort of accord can be reached."

"There is tremendous significance to the music that I play," Korm informed him.

"Yes! That's right! And the significance is that it's driving me crazy!"

"Gentlemen, please!" Trump clapped his hands sharply, and he looked in exasperation to Dini. "Let me get this straight. Mr. Cannelli lives above Korm, and Korm's music has been keeping him awake at night, and you can't separate them?"

"We don't have the room!" said Dini.

"I assume," said K'Ehleyr, addressing Korm, "that you are a member of the Consar discipline."

"You assume correctly," said Korm.

When Dini looked in confusion at the two, Khard explained, "The Consar discipline is a particular religious sect. They believe in making a joyous music to a particular—'muse' is the term you would use. The requirement is that it is made in the middle of the night, and the instrument of Korm's choice happens to be the yggim, which is somewhat similar to the Earth instrument you call drums."

"Terrific!" wailed Cannelli. "Just terrific! He has to get religion at night, and he's doing it by pounding away on the drums!"

"Certainly a compromise can be reached," said K'Ehleyr, although she didn't look too hopeful.

"Yes! It's a very simple compromise. He doesn't play his blasted music late at night, so that I can sleep! Easy compromise! Easy solution!"

"It is not that easy," said Khard.

But before he could continue, Worf said, "I do not understand the problem."

Korm frowned. "I do not see why not. It is fairly simple. Our religion dictates that music be played at that time so our muse can be lulled to sleep."

"By *drums?!*" wailed Cannelli. "What next? Explosions?"

"There is something that you have not allowed for, Korm," Worf told him.

"Oh really? And what might that be?"

"By my calculations," Worf punched some quick numbers into a computer padd, "when you are playing in the middle of the night here, it is, in fact, early morning on our home world. You have not allowed for the time difference."

Korm tried to come up with a reply to that, but nothing seemed to suggest itself immediately. He looked questioningly at Khard, who shrugged. "But—"

"There is no 'but,'" said Worf firmly. "I have made a thorough study of your religion. Consar inhabits the temples of the home world. Presuming that your music carries to her—and I am not disputing that it does—then you are, in fact, waking her up. You are doing her no favor at all."

The others were looking at him in amazement.

"The way I see it," Worf continued, "the only appropriate thing to do is to perform your music at the time corresponding to midnight on the home world. Correct?"

"I—I suppose." Korm looked uncertain, which was certainly an improvement over indignant.

"That being the case, I would recommend that you make your music at—let me see," and he punched in a few more calculations. "That would be fourteen hundred hours. Early afternoon. That would hardly serve as any sort of impediment to someone sleeping, I would think."

Silent looks were exchanged at the table. "Korm," said Khard cautiously. "Does this seem equitable to you?"

"I—believe it does," said Korm, sounding rather surprised over the entire turn that matters had taken.

"Mr. Cannelli?"

Cannelli spread his hands wide. "No problems here."

"Then that's that." Trump rose, shook Cannelli's hand, and nodded deferentially toward Korm. The two colonists walked out, looking at each other as if they were amazed that they weren't going to be fighting anymore.

"I admit," Khard said slowly, "I am impressed, Mr. Trump. Mr. Worf, you handled that quite skillfully."

K'Ehleyr, in spite of herself, found herself nodding. She quickly stopped.

"I understand Klingons," Worf told him. "And I understand Terrans. Between the two, there is little I cannot grasp."

"Is that so?" Khard appeared to consider this a moment. Then he said, "Mr. Trump, it is my opinion that we are not needed in these proceedings. I believe that Worf and K'Ehleyr should handle these matters."

There was a uniform chorus of "What?" from all concerned.

Utterly unphased, Khard continued, "Both of our groups are tired of looking at the two of us. Our effectiveness is somewhat limited in this situation. But word will spread quickly that Mr. Worf here handled the first of what will be many adjudicated disputes with relative ease. The Klingons will respect that. And the Terrans will respect that. I would like K'Ehleyr to remain, to serve as a representative from the Klingon Empire. Other than that, however, I see no need for anyone else in this room."

Dini was actually nodding. Trump was stroking his chin thoughtfully.

"I'm not certain I agree with that," K'Ehleyr began, casting a quick look at Worf.

"I do not recall asking whether you agreed with it or not," said Khard firmly. "Colonist I may be, K'Ehleyr, but I am your superior in rank and experience as well. I say how matters will proceed." He turned away from her, indicating that their conversation was over. "So, Dini—Trump—are we agreed?"

"All right. I'll give it a go," said Trump.

"Professor!" Worf was clearly stunned. "Do you think that is wise?"

"What's wrong, Mr. Worf?" asked Trump. "Are you telling me that you feel yourself incapable of handling this assignment?"

"No," said Worf quickly. "I can deal with whatever situation I am given. It is simply that—"

"Simply that what?" His face was a question mark.

"Nothing," said Worf, his voice dropping to a low growl.

"Good! Paul?"

Dini nodded. "All right. I'm not sure it's what I would have come up with myself, but if you two are certain—"

"Good!" Trump thudded his hands on the table top and stood. "It's settled then. Gentlemen?"

The others rose as well and they headed for the door. "Professor!" called Worf. "How long will we be required to be in charge of these—proceedings?"

Trump turned to face him and spread his hands wide. "Why, until they are done, Mr. Worf."

"We've had a large number of petty arguments, squabbles, and fights in the past week," Dini said. "Attempts by Khard and myself to smooth things out have been less effective than they could have been."

"Futile is what they have been," Khard told them bluntly. "Obviously, what was needed were some new faces. With any luck, we will have this colony a smoothly running enterprise in a week or two."

"I had scheduled far more time for Cannelli and Korm," said Dini. "Since you handled them so quickly, it will take me a few minutes to summon the next case. So you two relax for a few minutes, and then we'll have the next petitioners for righteous actions brought before you."

"Good job, Mr. Worf," said Trump. "You are doing Starfleet proud."

And the three of them walked out of the room, leaving Worf alone with K'Ehleyr.

"Steady, Zak. That's good. Now, lower it in gently."

The Brikar was staggering slightly under the weight

of his load, which happened to be a massive pulse generator the size of a boulder.

Several of the colonists, both Terran and Klingon,
were nodding approvingly, and making no effort to hide
how impressed they were. Tania, who was facing Zak,
had been moving backward. Now she had stopped
though, and her hands were mirroring Zak's careful la-
bors. "Sloooowwwwly," she said. "Verrryyy slowly.
We don't want to botch this up, Zak. This place powers
everything from food processors to planetary
defenses."

Zak allowed a brief grunt to escape his lips, but other
than that he did not acknowledge, in any way, the
weight of the component he was carrying.

The Starfleet Academy cadets were inside the main

power-source building, where the crystal-driven generators that supplied the colony with its energy were stored. The generators were not especially state of the art, but they got the job done. There were older, backup generators as well, stationed in a relatively small shack just outside the main supply plant. The hope, however, was that there would be no need to use them.

The large equipment that Zak was handling thumped squarely back into place. Only then did Zak let out a sigh, giving the slightest hint of just how much of a strain the thing had been on him. "Out of curiosity," he grunted, "wasn't there any way that you could have repaired this thing while it was still in its receptacle? Did I *have* to move the entire thing?"

"It was the only way to get at the connectors," she said. "That's why they kept having fluctuations in the energy flow; because the original connectors were faulty."

One of the Terran colonists on the tech crew stepped forward. "So this means that we don't have to worry about those spot blackouts anymore?"

"Right," said Tania. "What was happening was that you were managing to compensate for the outages by rerouting through other systems. But it was always temporary patches, and whenever you had the slightest overload, you'd blow out again. This beast," and she looked at the generator ruefully, "is not the greatest design. It's a powerful package, but not all the parts are as accessible as they should be. The couplings are designed to last for at least twenty years, but these were faulty and wore out in no time. Now lifting out the processor is fairly easy if you have anti-grav lifts—"

"Which we do not," acknowledged one of the Klingons, "since they didn't seem particularly necessary."

Tania turned to the tech crew. "All right. Fire 'er up. Let's see what we've got."

Several colonists headed over to the array of control panels that lined a nearby wall. They worked quickly and efficiently, which Tania was quite pleased to see. When she had first arrived to work with them on improving energy consumption, she had encountered bickering and hostility. The Klingon and Terran colonists seemed interested not so much in repairing what had gone wrong as assigning blame to someone for why something had gone wrong. It was not terribly constructive. Both groups had indulged in the unproductive pastime, and had even accused each other of mucking with the systems deliberately for some unknown purpose. What had prevented the situation from overloading was, quite simply, that neither group knew why the other would be interested in sabotaging the colony generators.

The fact was, as Tania discovered that *no one* had been mucking with anything; it was all normal equipment problems. Tania's brisk analysis of the situation and deft handling of repairs—aided and abetted by the might of Zak Kebron—had all of the colonists nodding their approval.

At that moment, Gowr and Kodash walked in. Gowr loudly announced, "All right, who is in charge here?"

The respective tech heads of the Klingon and Terran groups stepped forward. Gowr nodded and said, "We understand there has been some problems with power regulation. We are here to inspect it and help where we—"

"Not necessary," said Zak, unable to keep the smugness out of his voice. "It's already been attended to."

This prompted nothing but the deepest scowl possible from the two Klingons. "What do you mean, Brikar?" demanded Kodash.

Zak's face darkened and he took a step forward. Sensing possible difficulties, Tania moved in between Zak and the two Klingons. "He means," she said, "that, since you were busy elsewhere in the compound—taking care of, no doubt, important matters—we completed repairs on the generators. That should not be a problem, right? After all, we're all here to get things done."

"Not that you could possibly have taken care of this, even if you'd been of a mind to," Zak said.

Tania shot him an angry glance that seemed to shout, *Shut up, Zak!* If he noticed it, he didn't indicate it.

"What is that supposed to mean?" demanded Kodash. His fists seemed to be flexing and tightening.

Zak started to reply, but then he caught Tania's expression. He saw the anger in her face.

And he abruptly realized that he was sliding back into old habits. When he had first met Worf, he had taken every opportunity to bait him and provoke him. His deeply rooted prejudices against Klingons had come close to getting him kicked out of the Academy. Fortunately for all concerned—and most especially, himself—his time spent with Worf had made him realize that generalizing about any race as a whole was an inappropriate and ultimately ill-serving attitude to have. He had managed, over time, to overcome that anti-Klingon bias. Now he was simply going to have to get used to the notion of treating all Klingons with some measure of respect, even those he hadn't roomed with.

All this went through his mind in a few moments, and he framed a reply in his mind that would be polite to the Klingon emissaries.

Unfortunately, however, it was too late. Kodash had a reputation for being quick to anger, a reputation with which Zak was not familiar.

"Anything that you could accomplish, Starfleet man, is something that we could do as well," said Kodash angrily. "The superior attitude of the Brikar is almost as well known as the superior attitude of Starfleet itself."

The heads of the colonists were swinging back and forth, as if they were watching a brisk tennis match.

Zak bristled, finding it more and more difficult to rein himself in. "Listen, I am trying to be polite to you."

"Really?" Gowr contributed from behind the taller, more powerful Kodash. "I would hate to see you in action if you were trying to insult us."

"Gentlemen, please!" Tania said, trying to grab command of the situation. Although Tania was capable of wielding some measure of authority when circumstances were stable, calming a Klingon and Brikar down when they were this angry was simply beyond her abilities to do.

"You do not want me angry at you," said Zak dangerously. "Ask any of the individuals here. They have seen what I can do. They have seen my strength."

"Strength is not everything," scoffed Kodash. "There is speed, agility, talent and, most of all, intelligence."

"Oh really—?"

Tania put a hand on Zak's arm and said in a low voice, "Zak, let it go."

But he shook it off and continued dangerously, "If intelligence is such an important factor then where do you fit in?"

Kodash seemed to shake in place, his fists balled up and poised just over his belt buckle.

And then he charged at Zak.

Zak smiled, bracing himself, confident. He made no serious effort to block the Klingon's first punch, which he assumed would not hurt him at all.

He assumed incorrectly, however. From his belt buckle, Kodash had pulled a palm-sized neural stunner, and when his flat-handed smack struck Zak's chest, the Brikar felt a massive charge throughout his body. His tough hide provided some protection, but not one hundred percent. He staggered, trying to pull himself together.

Kodash, his powerful legs driving him forward, slammed into Zak like a battering ram. Zak smashed backward through the door, and Kodash was right after him.

CHAPTER

"So," Worf said after a moment that seemed to hang forever in the air. "You are K'Ehleyr."

"And you're Worf. Son of Mogh."

"Yes."

"So." She drummed her fingers on the conference table. "What is the son of a Klingon doing among sons of humans?"

"My duty," he replied crisply.

"As are we all," she acknowledged. "But where does your duty lie? That, to me, is an important question."

"That should be obvious."

"It isn't. Tell me, Worf, how did you come to be among these humans?"

She was looking at him with great interest, but there was still something about her that made Worf uncomfortable. Was she asking because she was interested for

herself? Or was she pumping him for information, for some reason?

Ultimately, he decided it made no difference. He had nothing to hide.

"My family was part of the research outpost on Khitomer."

"Historic Khitomer," she said, understanding. "The site of the great peace treaty of 2293. And the site of a major Romulan attack in 2346."

"You are quite conversant in history."

"It's always been an interest of mine." She studied him. "So you were there? During the attack?"

"Yes. I was much younger then."

"Obviously." She thought a moment. "My readings of the tragedy had always indicated that there were few survivors. You were one of the lucky ones, then?"

"All things considered, I did not feel very 'lucky' at the time. I was saved by a Starfleet officer, a human named Sergey Rozhenko. He brought me to live on the farm world of Gault, and eventually to Earth. He and his wife raised me as their own."

"Except that you do not identify yourself as Worf, son of Sergey Rozhenko, do you?"

"One cannot forget one's heritage," he replied.

"No. One cannot. That is why I am curious as to your allegiances. You were raised as a human, but you are quite obviously Klingon. So where are your priorities? Are you true to humans or Klingons?"

"I am true to myself," he replied. "If there is only one of me, then that is acceptable. If there is never another Klingon in Starfleet, then that, too, is acceptable. What would be unacceptable is to be divided in my loyalties."

"You're saying that you would be willing to fight against Klingons on the side of the Federation?"

He looked at her curiously. "Why should such a fight be necessary? We are allies now."

She stood and circled the room. "Worf, things change. Politics is a volatile discipline. We may all be friends and collaborators today, but we could be mortal enemies tomorrow. If you are hanging your peace of mind on the status quo, you could very easily find yourself in a more difficult situation than you ever anticipated. And what will you do then, Worf, son of Mogh?"

He was silent for a moment. Then he said, "I will do what is right. I do not think that more could be expected from anyone."

She was about to reply, when suddenly they heard a commotion from outside. Worf, to his distress, recognized at least one of the voices clearly.

Worf was on his feet and vaulted over the table, getting to the door ahead of K'Ehleyr. He charged out and was appalled—while, unfortunately, not surprised—by what he saw.

Zak and Kodash were struggling in the middle of the central square of the colony. Colonists were gathering, pointing and shouting, but no one was getting close to the combatants. It was understandable that the colonists were keeping their distance, because the Klingon and Brikar clearly meant business.

Kodash had a choke hold on Zak, and once again applied the neural stunner to him. The Brikar twisted and writhed in Kodash's grip. Then he managed to get leverage, and he broke free, shoving Kodash away. Before Kodash could recover, Zak stepped forward quickly and slammed Kodash in the chest. Kodash went down and Zak lunged toward him. The Klingon barely managed to get out of the way in time.

The irony of the situation did not escape Worf. When he had first encountered Zak Kebron, the two of them had come to blows. They had been separated—by Starfleet security guards—before they tore off each other's heads. Now Worf found himself in the bizarre position of being peacemaker.

He shoved his way in between the two of them, ignoring the sudden feeling that he was taking his life in his hands. Regardless, he had to bring this to an immediate end.

"Stop it!" he thundered. "Both of you!"

"This isn't your concern, Worf!" said Zak. "Besides, he started it!"

"Me?" retorted Kodash. "You were the one who—"

"I do not care who started it!" snapped Worf. "All I know is that I am ending it. You will immediately cease hostilities!"

"Or what?" sneered Kodash. "Or you will make me? I would like to see you try."

"I am sure that you would," said Worf. "But I am not going to."

"Are you afraid?" Kodash challenged him. "Has being part of Starfleet made you a coward?"

"You see!" said Zak. "That's the kind of thing he was doing before!"

"No, it has not made me a coward," Worf told him. "Nor has it made me a blustering fool."

"You call me a fool?" snapped Kodash.

But K'Ehleyr had now come up behind Worf. "You assumed that he was referring to you, Kodash," she said sharply. "And I wouldn't blame him if he had been. Now stand down."

Kodash glared at her. "If you had not been made leader of this mission—"

"But I was, Kodash. I was. Debate me all you wish, but I have the final authority. Stand down, I said. Is that clear?"

It seemed as if Kodash was weighing his options. What were the opportunities for directly attacking K'Ehleyr. Or Worf. Or Zak, for that matter, who had been the reason for this entire thing.

Finally, he sighed loudly and angrily enough to get his thoughts across, and then he said, "As you wish, K'Ehleyr. I," and he tossed a significant glance at Worf, "know my duty."

"Good for you," said Worf.

The colonists, realizing that the show was over, began to drift away. Both Zak and Kodash moved away as well, although in different directions and not without tossing angry glances at each other. Tania, who had followed the course of the fight, looked a bit apprehensive as she walked up to Worf. "You handled that perfectly," she told him.

"How did it happen?" demanded Worf.

She told him quickly, and concluded, "It was just a good thing that you were here, that's all."

He was about to tell her that, obviously, she had done all that she could. But then he noticed the way that K'Ehleyr was watching him, as if she were judging him. She was the leader of her group, just as he was the leader of his. And he suddenly felt a great deal of pressure, for no reason that he could understand.

He scowled more darkly than Tania had ever seen, which puzzled her. And then, to her astonishment, he said, "You should have not let it happen, Tania."

"Me?" She tried not to laugh. "How was I supposed to stop it? They would have stepped on me."

"You were overseeing an engineering function. That makes it your responsibility. I suggest that, in the future, you make certain to keep a firmer hand on situations *before* they erupt into violence. Is that understood?"

She studied him with a curious tilt of her head. "Oh yes, *sir,* Mr. Worf. What could I have been thinking? In the future, Mr. Worf, I shall stay right on top of it, even if it might get me killed, because I wouldn't want to disappoint you, Mr. Worf, *sir.*"

She turned on her heel and walked off.

He sensed, rather than saw, K'Ehleyr nodding behind

him. "You were absolutely right, Worf. She handled that entire situation poorly. She can't let people under her command get out of control that way. If we do not have control, if we do not have discipline, then we have nothing. Don't you agree?"

"Of course," he said with difficulty.

She paused a moment and then asked, "Do you have any intention of reporting her to your superiors?"

"No. I do not think that is necessary."

"She was rather insubordinate, if you ask me—"

He turned to face her and said pointedly, "I did not ask you. Come, the next people seeking adjudication should be along shortly. We should not be late."

He headed back into the building, with a curious and silent K'Ehleyr behind him.

CHAPTER

Several days had passed, and Paul Dini and Khard had decided that a celebration was in order for the two teams. Nothing fancy, of course, for they were colonists of simple means. But it was more than adequate.

Unfortunately, the Klingon and Terran definitions of what constituted quality food were very different. So Dini was serving up a meal that was somewhere in between which was, ultimately, not totally satisfactory to anyone but not completely inedible to anyone.

The dinner was taking place in one of the multipurpose buildings. It served as Dini's office, not to mention his quarters. It also had a large dining area for guests, which is where they were at the moment.

In the best tradition of Camelot, the table in the dining quarters was round so that there was no head of the table. Individuals could sit wherever they felt comfortable, and no particular importance was assigned to any one position. Nevertheless, they did tend to cluster by groups. The Starfleet cadets sat with each other, as did the Klingons. Professor Trump, however, made sure to position himself so that he was a physical bridge between the groups: Soleta sat to his left, while Gowr was on his right.

Worf watched with admiration as Trump conversed in a comfortable manner with the Klingon delegation.

Soleta was looking around. "Where is McHenry?" she asked.

Worf now saw that, indeed, there was no sign of Mark McHenry. He frowned and said, "He is not here yet?"

"It would seem not," said Soleta.

Tania turned and looked at Worf, and she said pointedly, "Do you want me to go find him for you, *Mr. Worf?*"

The slight edge in her voice was apparent to everyone at the table. Worf shifted uncomfortably in his chair and said, "No. That will not be necessary. I will locate him."

"Are you not capable of keeping track of your own people, Mr. Worf?" asked Gowr.

Before Worf could answer, Trump said, "Starfleet personnel are capable of keeping track of themselves, Gowr. Mr. McHenry is, very likely, involved in helping some colonists with a difficult situation and, as a result, is unaware of the time. Mr. Worf, however, is going to be kind enough to find him and remind him of the lateness of the hour. Correct, Mr. Worf?"

"Absolutely," said Worf. And then he added, "And Ms. Tobias will be assisting me."

He looked straight at Tania, and now it was her turn to feel uncomfortable. But she hesitated only a moment before getting to her feet and saying politely, "Yes, sir." And she followed Worf out the door.

The moment they were outside and in the street, Worf turned to her and said in irritation, "Would you mind telling me what the problem is?"

"Me? What problem could I possibly have?"

"You have been cold and formal with me for several days."

"A subordinate is supposed to be formal with a commanding officer. Didn't you know that?"

She started to walk away from him, and he took her by the arm and swung her around. "Tania, I thought we were friends. . . ."

Her chin twitched and she said angrily, "Yeah, I thought we were friends, too. Then you decided to ream me out just to impress your Klingon girlfriend—"

"She is not my girlfriend!" Worf said indignantly. "And I was right to say something to you; you should have stopped things from going as far as they did. It is a matter of responsibility—"

"No, Worf, it's a matter of respect. And your need for getting K'Ehleyr's respect became more important than your consideration for me."

"I have the utmost consideration for you," he said stiffly. "You are simply having difficulty dealing with criticism—"

"No, I'm not," she shot back. "What I'm angry

about is how you said it, rather than what you said. If you've got a problem with me, or how I'm doing something, then you discuss it with me privately. You got that? You and me, the two of us. All disagreements should always be handled that way: in private. That way the subordinate isn't made to feel that she's being held up to public ridicule in front of her peers. And she can defend herself to her commanding officer without it coming across as insubordination.''

"That is not how Klingons do things. You speak your mind and answer for the consequences of your actions. Whoever might be standing around is irrelevant.''

"Well, here's a news flash for you, Worf. You're not part of a Klingon crew. You're part of a Starfleet crew, or at least that's what you're training to become. And if you're having trouble with that, then maybe you *should* go off and join your Klingon friends.''

Worf was stunned by her reaction. It seemed out of proportion to the incident that had sparked it.

But he knew that it wouldn't hurt him to be a bit more flexible every now and then.

In as soft a voice as he could, he said, ''Tania, I am sorry. I am very sorry that I have upset you, and I will do whatever I can to make sure it does not happen again.''

She turned and studied him, in the fading daylight. ''Really? You mean it?''

''Of course I mean it,'' he said. And truly, he did. He was aware that there were subtleties to human emotions that he was not yet grasping, indeed, perhaps would never grasp. But to remain stubborn in all matters until he did understand them—whenever that time might come—would leave behind him a long road of hurt emotions and feelings. That was no way to live.

She finally smiled, and then she stepped forward and hugged him briefly. "Thank you," she said. "And—I'm sorry, too."

"For what?"

"You know."

"Yes. Of course," he said stiffly, in fact not knowing but deciding that it was better to just nod and accept it. "That is quite all right. So—on to the other pressing difficulty of the evening. Where is McHenry?"

"Actually, that's going to be an easy one." She pointed. "There."

Sure enough, the redheaded cadet was walking across the street, looking upward, holding the tricorder that he had won during the poker game on the *Repulse*. He was smiling in a lopsided manner, seemingly delighted with his new "toy." At the same time he was displaying his remarkable knack for keeping track of many things at the same time, because he was unerringly steering himself around passersby without giving them so much as a glance.

"Mac!" called out Tania.

He glanced her way and then, still looking at the tricorder, made his way over to her and Worf. "Hi," he said.

"Aren't you expected somewhere?" she asked, her arms folded.

He regarded her curiously. "Is this a trick question?"

"We were supposed to be meeting with the others for dinner," Worf reminded him.

McHenry looked surprised. "Is it eighteen hundred hours already?"

"Yes."

"Huh. Now isn't that annoying. I programmed the tricorder to remind me automatically when it was time for the get-together. And here it didn't. Maybe there's something wrong with it." He paused, and then said, "I know . . ."

"He is going to hit it again," sighed Worf.

It was how Mark McHenry dealt with any piece of equipment that seemed to be giving him problems. It was annoying for two reasons: First, because it showed an utter disregard for the delicacy of the technology involved; and second, because—aggravatingly—it always seemed to work.

"Wait, let me have a look at it," Tania started to say, but it was too late. McHenry gave it a shot in the side and then the tricorder obediently beeped at him.

"Ah," he smiled, a direct contrast to Tania's scowl. "There. The timer has . . ."

But suddenly he was frowning, an expression that rarely crossed his face. "Where'd that come from?" he asked.

"What? Where?"

McHenry didn't answer Worf's question. Instead he suddenly craned his neck skyward, aiming his tricorder.

And then, galvanized in abrupt action, he shouted, *"Get to cover!"* He bolted toward Paul Dini's place, leaving a puzzled Worf and Tania where they were.

"What's with him?" asked Tania.

Suddenly the air seemed to crackle around them, and the ground exploded.

Tania and Worf were hurled in different directions. Worf slammed into a nearby dormitory. From within he heard shouts, cries of confusion. High above the clouds, beyond the point where he could see the origin of the attack, beams of destructive force rained down. The rough paths through the town were chewed up by the energy blasts. One of the blasts struck a warehouse, where grain—the extremely adaptable quadrotriticale that the colonists were in the process of growing on the planet's arid surface—was stored. The building exploded, and grain was hurled everywhere in vast showers.

Worf scrambled to his feet just in time to see a huge mountain of grain come pouring down on Tania. She reached out to him, but she was too far away, and within an eyeblink she was buried.

He charged forward, uncaring of the danger. All around him lights suddenly went out, and he was aware that the main generator, and quite possibly the backup, had been struck. But that didn't matter to him at the moment. None of it mattered except rescuing Tania.

He dove in and started shoveling grain out of the way, digging down toward Tania as quickly as he could. He shouted her name, told her to hold on. It seemed forever, and he wasn't finding any hint of her. He was starting to despair of saving her, and he was even flashing back momentarily to that traumatic moment when,

as a young Klingon, he had been buried alive during the Romulan attack on Khitomer.

But then his hand closed around a wrist, and he gripped it firmly. A hand closed around his upper arm. With only seconds to act, he pulled as hard as he could, hoping that he wouldn't simply yank her arm out of the socket. At first there was no movement, but then he staggered slightly as she shifted within. He took a step back, and then another, and then Tania Tobias slid out of her entrapment. She was gasping, coughing up grain while trying to suck air greedily into her lungs. Every inch of her was covered with grain, and she was clawing blindly at the air.

"You are all right!" he called to her, trying to cut through her panic. "You are all right!"

She said nothing at first, her chest heaving. She coughed, sending a mouthful of grain spewing onto the ground.

"Tania—"

She nodded her head, acknowledging his voice. "I know," she whispered hoarsely. "I know I'm all right. What happened? What the heck happened?"

"We are being attacked."

She looked up at him with a glazed expression. "No kidding."

He stood and swung her up into his arms. "Don't try to talk," he warned her.

She nodded, taking him at his word.

He ran as fast as he could, her additional weight not slowing him at all. Within moments he arrived back at Paul Dini's command center.

The dining table had changed function significantly. Before it was the place where food was served. Now all the diners were crouched under it, seeking shelter from pieces of the ceiling that were raining down from the attack.

The only ones who weren't crouched under there were McHenry and Zak. Both were in the process of heading for the door with the clear intention of going after Worf and Tania. When Worf entered, Zak immediately ran to him and shielded the two of them with his own body. "Are you all right?" he shouted.

"Yes," said Worf, lowering Tania to the ground. "At least, as fine as we can be, considering that someone is trying to kill us."

The pounding, however, seemed to have stopped. Immediately everyone scattered out from under the table, and Dini called out, "I'm heading to the Monitor building!"

"I will go with you," snapped Worf. "Kebron, McHenry, with me." And then, realizing that he might have overstepped his authority, since he was barking orders while the professor was around, he turned to Trump belatedly for authority.

But Trump just nodded confirmation.

"What about me?" said Soleta. She did not display irritation in being left behind, but clearly it was on her mind.

"You are the closest thing we have to a doctor with us," replied Worf. "Take care of Tania. We will be back shortly."

"I'm coming as well," K'Ehleyr now said. "And Gowr will accompany me."

"What about me?" demanded Kodash.

"You stay here."

"Why?"

"Because I am tired of you getting into fights with the Brikar every time you are together. We do not need bickering now; we need cooperation."

Worf growled, "All right then. Let us go."

Tania watched as Worf, K'Ehleyr and the others went out the door. She had been laid flat on the ground, and she thudded her head lightly in frustration.

The simple fact was that—aside from the fact that she cared for Worf—she disliked the feeling that there was some sort of "competition" going on for Worf's loyalties. He was Starfleet, one of them. But now that he was around Klingons, was he feeling torn? When the time came to leave Dantar would the Starfleet cadets be departing with one less member than when they arrived?

The idea that the Klingons might be able to offer Worf a sense of friendship, of spiritual communion, that no one at the Academy could, was extremely aggravating to Tania. One always wants to "be there" for one's friends. And to find that you are coming up short. . . .

It was not a feeling she cherished.

Kodash, for his part, spat out a curse, and then grabbed a tricorder and stomped out the door.

Soleta didn't know where he was going, nor did she particularly care. She had her own concerns. Although science was her specialty, she had had some training

back on Vulcan in the healing arts, since her parents were both medical practitioners. Naturally the Vulcan physiology was different from humans, but a broken bone was still a broken bone.

She did not find any such injuries in Tania, which was fortunate. But Tobias was still clearly upset and frustrated. Her heart rate was accelerated and her pulse was pounding so fiercely that Soleta thought Tania might pass out.

"Lie back," she said softly. "Relax."

"Relax? Are you *nuts?* How am I supposed to relax when—"

Soleta's fingers brushed Tania's forehead. Ever so faintly, ever so slightly, her mind touched Tania's, and she said again, "Relax."

Tania's head obediently sagged back. Her eyes closed, she said distantly, "You know, I really should relax."

"I think that would be an excellent idea," Soleta agreed.

CHAPTER

"It's not good."

The Monitor building was a central point where, as the name suggested, all activities and systems throughout the colony were monitored. There were computer setups, as well as readouts on the various operations that kept the colony going. And right now the head monitor, a woman named Greenberg, was less than optimistic.

She was pointing to one screen after another. Several were blank, two were filled with static. And the ones that were still working were giving her readouts that weren't promising.

"The backup generator is on-line now," she said, "so we've got some power going. But our long-range sensors are down, not to mention our planetary defense systems."

"The defense systems being . . . ?" asked K'Ehleyr.

"Two standing phaser cannons."

"And . . . ?"

"And that's it," said Greenberg.

K'Ehleyr looked appalled. "That's *it?* You have nothing beyond two standing phaser cannons?"

"What about those?" Worf interrupted, pointing to one screen that displayed a landing field with several small ships squatting there, inactive. "Are there weapons aboard them?"

Dini shook his head. "No. Those are just simple transport ships. Emergency vehicles, that sort of thing."

"Which they did not touch." Worf stroked his chin. "Why do you think that is?"

"Likely it's the same reason they didn't simply destroy this settlement," said Kebron. "They want to preserve whatever they can for their own use."

"Is that your best guess, Brikar?" Gowr said, making no effort to hide his contempt. "Do not be ridiculous. They are just toying with us, that is all."

"You think you know everything, don't you, Klingon?"

"One does not have to know everything in order to know far more than you—"

"Stop it! Both of you!" snapped Dini. "This is abs—"

"You hit them."

It was McHenry who had spoken. They all turned and stared at the softspoken astronavigator, who was in turn looking at his tricorder.

"What do you mean? Who hit who?"

"The phaser cannons," McHenry replied. "The attack exhibited a drop in emissions that would be consistent with the sudden energy loss if a direct hit were sustained. Obviously the cannons got off a few automatic shots before they were put out of commission.''

"How could you tell that from a tricorder?'' demanded Gowr. "It is impossible! No tricorder would have that kind of range!''

"This one does,'' said McHenry calmly.

Abruptly the door burst open, and standing there was Kodash. K'Ehleyr looked at him angrily and snapped, "What are you doing here? I told you to—''

"I know what you told me,'' he shot back. "And while I was waiting, I ran an analysis on the particle emanations from the blast points. Would you like to know what I discovered?'' He stabbed a finger at the Starfleet cadets. "The weapons used were standard phasers of Federation design! We were fired on by a Federation ship! Probably Starfleet!''

"That's ridiculous!'' snapped Zak. "Why would a Starfleet ship attack the colony?''

"Because there are Klingons here! Why else?''

"That is an insane accusation,'' Worf informed him.

"Is it? Why so? It is a perfect way to dispose of a bunch of stinking Klingons, right?'' said Gowr contemptuously, taking up Kodash's train of thought. "No one would ever suspect that the Federation would be so depraved as to destroy their own people to get at the Klingon colonists.''

"You know as little about the Federation as you do about all other things,'' Zak said, and his three-fingered hands started to ball up into fists.

"Stop this insanity, immediately!'' said Worf. K'Ehleyr

was likewise trying to calm down her people. Dini, satisfied that Worf and K'Ehleyr were managing to keep a lid on things, was conferring with Greenberg about needed repairs.

Meantime, McHenry was calmly feeding information from the tricorder into the computer base. "If you'd like," he said, "I can get you an image of our attacker."

"Yes, by all means," sneered Gowr. "Let us see the face of the enemy."

"Your attacks on the reputation of the Federation are truly pathetic," Worf said.

At that moment an image appeared on the screen, and there were gasps all around the room.

Slowly, Zak Kebron turned to face the astonished expressions of K'Ehleyr, Gowr, and Kodash. "Correct me if I am wrong," said Zak. "But that would appear to be a Klingon vessel. True or false?"

"It—it is a trick!" snapped Gowr defensively.

"Is it now?" Zak's voice became louder, angrier. "And who is it who is being tricked, eh? Perhaps every colonist on this world is the butt of your curious little joke!"

"I am telling you, it is not true! Why would a Klingon vessel fire upon this world?"

"Oh, well!" crowed Zak. "You found it *so* easy to believe that the Federation would have its reasons. And now you're telling me that a peoples with a history of treachery are incapable of having some sort of dark, sinister motivation for the things they do—"

"That is enough! Both of you!" snapped Worf.

And K'Ehleyr echoed, "Yes, more than enough."

Worf continued. "We do not know what is going on up there, so we must—"

"The important thing"—Dini interrupted—"is to defend ourselves should this attacker return!"

"He'll most likely return," said McHenry calmly. "We damaged him, but I doubt it's something he can't repair. And then he'll be back with guns blazing, ready to blow us off the face of the planet." After a moment's thought he added, "That's a worst-case scenario, of course."

"We could evacuate," offered Greenberg.

"The moment we leave the planet's surface, we would be targets for them," said Worf. "We've only got one chance: We have to repair the phaser cannons."

"But they've been destroyed!" Greenberg pointed out.

"Yes, I know," Worf said sarcastically. "I doubt they would need repair if they had not been."

"It's not possible!" said Dini flatly.

"Of course it is possible. The only question is whether it is possible within whatever time we may have left."

"I think you'll be needing my help, then."

It was Tania who had spoken. She was standing in the doorway looking a bit woozy, but otherwise determined. Behind her were Soleta and Professor Trump.

"You should be resting!" said Worf sternly.

"If I get buried under two tons of rubble, I'll have all eternity to rest."

"She's fine, Worf. Good enough for what needs to be done, at any rate," Soleta assured him.

"All right. Fine. Let's get over to the planetary defense systems—what is left of them, anyway. That has to be our first priority—that, and getting the main generators back on-line. We will need the additional power they'll provide."

Everyone filed out, with the last to go being Worf and Zak. But Worf stopped his roommate, and when he spoke it was with a dark scowl. "What was that supposed to mean?" he demanded.

"What was what supposed to mean?"

"That comment about 'A peoples with a history of treachery.'"

"Oh, that." Kebron gave a dismissive wave. "He angered me, that's all. I certainly hope you're not taking that personally."

"How else am I supposed to take it? I thought we were past all that, Zak."

"We are. You and I are. But you're not like them—"

"No, Zak. I am like them. I am far more like them than I am like you, or Tania, or anyone else here. And I will appreciate it if you do not slander my people in that manner."

"Your people," said Zak, bristling, "have a history of—"

But then he stopped.

"Fine," he said. "Fine. I see no point to carrying on

90

with this, especially since we will most likely be dead within a few hours."

"If we are fortunate," replied Worf, "we will survive long enough to kill each other."

"One can only hope."

CHAPTER

11

"Ohhhh dear."

The comment was from Paul Dini, and the sight that he was viewing was not good.

The impact of the blasts had literally knocked the two massive phaser cannons over. Each of the weapons was about twenty feet high, and incredibly heavy. They were long and streamlined, so large that they had seats at the end for operators to sit in if they wished to target manually. When mounted upright (as they had been shortly before) they were on swiveling turrets, their vicious muzzles aimed skyward through slots in the building's domed ceiling.

Worf, Dini, Trump, Zak, K'Ehleyr, and Kodash examined the situation with dismay. A number of other colonists were around as well, looking in frustration at the situation.

"We need pulleys, some sort of lever system," suggested K'Ehleyr.

"There isn't time!" said Dini.

And then one of the colonists was heard to shout, "It's all your fault!"

It was a Terran colonist who had spoken, and he was addressing one of his Klingon co-workers. The Klingon's mouth drew back in a snarl as the Terran said, "It was a Klingon ship that did this!"

"It was Federation weapons that did this!" snapped back the Klingon.

Trump looked questioningly at Dini, who shrugged helplessly. "It's a small colony. Word gets around quickly here."

In the meantime more heated words were being exchanged, and then abruptly two groups of colonists charged each other, Klingons on one side and Terrans on the other. Months of frustration and anger were now fueled by terror of their predicament, and they struck out at the only enemy that they could get their hands on: each other.

It took the Federation and Klingon teams long moments to pull the warring factions apart, and Trump abruptly spoke in a voice so loud, so sweeping, that it demanded immediate attention.

"You pathetic fools!" he boomed. "Is your hatred and hostility more important to you than your own survival? The enemy isn't down here. He's up there! He's effecting repairs on his ship at this very moment, and there's every chance that—whatever his reasons for wanting to attack you—he's going to come back and finish the job! Now are you going to make his chore that much easier for him? Or are you going to give an accounting of yourselves? Show him what it means to take on the combined efforts of the Federation and the Klingon Empire! I came here concerned about the future of Klingon and Federation co-ventures. I tend to think that your major consideration should be concern about your own futures, which may not be measured much beyond the next few minutes!''

And suddenly, to Worf's astonishment, Trump yanked small hand phasers from his tunic. He stepped forward, shoved one into the hand of the nearest Terran colonist—who just happened to be Cannelli—and another into the hands of a Klingon, who just happened to be Korm. Then he stepped back and said, ''Fine! Go ahead! Shoot each other! See if I care!'' And when they paused, looking momentarily confused, Trump said even more forcefully, ''Go on! Do it! Each of you let the other know how tough he is! How right he is! Go on and let each other have it! You know it's what you want to do! So do it!''

Korm and Cannelli looked at each other, and looked at the phasers in their hands.

''Well?'' spat out Trump. ''What are you waiting for, eh?''

''I am not,'' said Korm tersely, ''going to give whoever is shooting down at us the satisfaction of dying without a fight. And shooting Cannelli here is not going to accomplish that end.''

''I'm not going to shoot if *he's* not going to shoot,'' said Cannelli. ''That's not the way I operate.''

''Fine,'' said Trump. He grabbed the phasers out of their hands and said, ''Now let's get to work and do this before it all becomes moot. You people over there, look at getting the relays back on-line. The rest of you, do whatever it takes to get the things upright and mounted again. *Let's move!"*

Everyone jumped to work, but Worf and K'Ehleyr took a moment to sidle over to Trump. "You took a rather large chance there, Professor," said Worf in a low voice.

"Not really," replied Trump, holding one of the phasers in his palm. "The phasers were empty; out of power. See?" And he turned and thumbed the trigger.

A bright blue bolt shot out of the phaser, drilling a hole in the wall just to the right of Zak Kebron's head. He whirled in surprise.

K'Ehleyr and Worf gaped at a chagrined Trump.

"Ooops," was all he could think of to say.

Tania was surveying the generator room with dismay. Various phaser blasts had done a job on relays and systems lines. With her going over the system were Soleta, Gowr, Khard, and McHenry.

"Here's where we have to put top priority," called out Soleta. She was pointing to a particular area on an electronic schematic that had been called up on one of the functioning computer screens. "This is the subsystems that powers the phaser cannons. If we don't reestablish this link, then none of the rest of it is going to matter."

"All right," said Tania crisply. "Mac, Gowr, we work on getting the generator up and running. Soleta, you and Khard get started on reestablishing the link."

There were noises from outside, the sounds of arguing. Colonists were shouting at each other. Khard went to the door and bellowed, "We could use some help in here! Which are you more interested in? Arguing, or saving your miserable hides?"

Within moments there were a half-dozen extra hands in the generator room, the "miserable hide" contingent apparently far outweighing the "arguing" contingent.

Somewhere high above the surface of Dantar IV, the crew of a ship finished repairs, and turned their attention back toward the planet's surface.

Through gritted teeth, Worf grunted, "Come on! Put your backs into it!"

The cumbersome phaser cannon was at a 45-degree angle and teetering. The only thing stopping it from falling was the combined strength of the cadets, the Klingons, and a number of colonists.

Zak and Kodash were side by side, pushing with all their considerable strength. Kodash tossed off a glance at Zak and grunted, "I heard that Brikar was supposed to have—some muscle to them—"

"More than enough—to match you—Klingon," snarled Zak.

"It's falling!" shouted Trump, who was not pushing but instead directing the efforts of those who were. "Watch it! Brace yourselves!"

But the team refused to let it happen. They redoubled their efforts, straining beyond the limits they thought they had. And slowly, ever so slowly, the phaser cannon inched upward, upward . . .

And then, so quickly that they couldn't quite believe it, it thudded into place back in its fixture. For a panicked moment it started to topple the other way, but just as quickly it righted itself and sat there, serenely in its place.

"All right! Get it on-line!" Worf quickly tapped his comm badge. "Worf to Tobias. How is it going, Tania?"

In the generator room, Tania was desperately checking over systems. "I'm not sure," she said. "Ask me in about ten seconds. Mac! Gowr! Are we ready to try and bring her back on-line?"

The two of them, along with some colonists, were doing last-minute checks. "I think we have a good shot at it," said Mac confidently. "Of course, let's be reasonable—we also have a good shot at blowing the entire generator sky high if the dampers don't hold and we get a feedback. So it really depends what you're up for, I guess."

"Swell. Everyone—back away!" The others did so, although it was just a courtesy warning on her part. For all she knew, if the dampers indeed did not hold, it might blow up the generator along with roughly a square kilometer of prime Dantar territory. But she saw no choice. She held her breath, tapped in a few last-minute commands, and then pulled a lever.

The lever slammed into place with a loud *ga-chunk*, and for a moment nothing seemed to be happening. And then, like the sound of a thousand powerful tigers all purring at once, the generator roared back to life.

A ragged cheer went up.

"Worf! We're up and running!" crowed Tania. "How are you there?"

In the phaser building, Worf turned to K'Ehleyr, who was heading up the systems operations. "The generator is running. We have power."

"Not here we don't," said K'Ehleyr bleakly. "I'm still reading systems zero."

"Tania! We are still dead here!"

In the generator room, Tania muttered a curse and swung down from her perch in the upper reaches of the generator. "Soleta! What's keeping that systems link-up? They haven't got power at the phaser cannon!"

"Almost done running a subsystems check. Ah!"

"What's 'ah'?"

"Found where the breakdown in the linkage is. It's in conduit five, section Thirteen-B."

"Can you route around it?"

"No," said Soleta. "I'll have to do it manually." She crossed the room quickly and pulled up a ventway that led into the power conduit. "Get me a tool pack, quickly."

"Let me do it," Tania began.

But Soleta shook her head. "No offense, Tania, but this will require a cool head. You are a valuable engineer, but you have the unfortunate tendency to let yourself become too upset. That is not a consideration where I am concerned. Besides, you will be just as nec-

essary here to monitor the systems and feed power to the weapons.

"Thank you," that last comment directed to Gowr who handed her a tool kit. "I shall be back shortly."

Gowr seemed to hesitate a moment, and then he grudgingly said, "Good luck."

"Luck?" Soleta eyed him curiously. "What an utterly irrelevant concept."

And then she vanished into the conduit, buckling the kit around her waist.

It was a narrow squeeze, but nothing that she could not overcome. She slid along quickly, her elbows pulling her forward, and she studied the array of circuitry around her. The conduit led directly to the weapons array, feeding power through, and somewhere there had been a breakdown in that connector. She had to repair it, and quickly.

Her comm link was open, and she spoke with calm, authoritative tones. "I am approaching the source of the trouble. I have reached section thirteen-A . . . section thirteen-B. I have arrived at the trouble spot." She held a glowtorch up, studying the connectors. "It would appear that the attack managed to overload one of the couplings. It should not take long to repair with a phaser-solder."

"Then do it already," came Tania's voice over the comm link.

Soleta raised an eyebrow even as she reached out and brought out a solder. "That *was* my intention."

She started to work quickly, efficiently.

And then she heard it. The sounds of phaser blasts ripping across the landscape aboveground.

"That," she said, "is unfortunate timing."

CHAPTER

Utterly confident of the colony's inability to defend itself, the attacking ship dropped closer to the planet's surface to commence another attack.

Destruction rained down, and Worf was bellowing into the comm link, as explosions erupted all around them, "Tania! We could really use power to the weapons about now!"

Tania, in turn, called into her own comm link, "Soleta! Move it!"

Soleta, for her part, heard the sounds of the firing, the screaming, the running feet. She did not, however, let it distract her from the meticulous performance of her job. "Just another few moments," she said calmly.

"We may not *have* another few moments!" Tania's voice came over the comm link.

In the weapons room, meantime, Worf turned to K'Ehleyr and called, "Any change in the readings?"

K'Ehleyr, at the firing and targeting controls, said, "No! We still have no power!"

And suddenly the building shook as a stray blast struck overhead.

K'Ehleyr looked up just in time to see a huge chunk of the ceiling plummeting toward her. And then a body slammed into her, knocking her aside. It was Professor Trump moving as quickly as he could, the urgency of the moment galvanizing him into action.

It was not, however, enough to keep him moving. He cried out as the ceiling caved in on him.

And then Zak Kebron was there, his massive and sturdy body outstretched over the professor. The rest of the crashing rubble cascaded down and off Zak's sturdy body, sparing the professor from further injury. What he did sustain, however, was more than enough to render him unconscious.

"Get him to safety!" called out Worf over the sounds of the phaser blasts from above.

"Safety? There is no safety!" shot back Kodash.

Worf did not reply. Instead he leaped up toward the targeting systems.

There was a roar from overhead. Through the gaping hole in the roof they could see the ship with their own eyes now, wings outstretched in the distinctive Klingon style. Undoubtedly their sensors had informed them that the planetary defense systems had no power to them. The colony world of Dantar was hopelessly crippled, and the invaders were about to deliver the final blow.

"Tania!" shouted Worf on the comm link.

"Soleta!" shouted Tania on the comm link.

And in the conduit Soleta made a final connection. All around her the power grids roared to life.

As calmly as if she were announcing the weather, Soleta said, "The couplings are alive and hot. Repeat, you're hot. Fire when ready."

Worf had been staring at the power readouts fiercely, as if trying to will them to life. The automatic target locks had the attacker dead in its sights, but there was no power to fuel the phaser cannon. And then suddenly the readings which had been lodged firmly at the bottom of the red zone skyrocketed to the top of the green, with "READY" indicator lights flashing.

He heard Tania's triumphant shout of "Worf! We're hot! Do it!"

Bolts screamed down from overhead as Worf slammed his fist on the trigger mechanism. The phaser cannon shrieked, deafening the people who were standing too close. But their shouts were not heard over the screech of the unleashed energy.

The attacker had a split-second warning when the phaser cannon came on-line, and that was nowhere near enough time to compensate. The cannon blast lanced across the ship's stern, ripping through the shield like tissue paper because of the close range. There was a brief moment when the power level dropped, and Worf fought down a wave of panic. But the system buffers that Tania had installed kicked in, preventing an overload, and the phaser cannon surged with renewed life.

Another powerful beam sliced through the right nacelle, shearing it free from the rest of the ship. The attacker spun hopelessly out of control, angling toward the desert. Long moments later the sound of a deafening crash echoed across the surface of Dantar IV, metal twisting in on itself.

A raucous cheer went up from everyone in the cannon housing. But it was quickly stilled as they heard the sounds of sobbing and cries from the colonists outside, and the air became filled with the smell of burning and a thick cloud of black smoke.

"Worf!" called out K'Ehleyr. He went over and knelt down next to her. She was cradling the bleeding head of Professor Trump in her lap, and she looked up at Worf worriedly.

"If he doesn't get medical attention immediately, I don't think he's going to make it."

"Medical attention is going to be a problem," said Dini, coming over. "The infirmary was one of the first things to be hit in the initial raid. I don't even want to think what's left of it by this point. Probably nothing."

Zak looked at Worf and said what they already knew: "We're not out of trouble yet, are we?"

And Worf shook his head. "No. Not by a long shot."

There was a sense of barely controlled panic in the air.

Everywhere buildings were burning and people were screaming for help. In the back of Worf's mind, as he carried a helpless little girl to safety, he felt himself flashing back again to Khitomer. Back then he had viewed the world through the eyes of a child; now he was grown, but the view from maturity was not much of an improvement.

With everyone pitching in, they managed to control the fires, and pull the people out from their temporary prisons of fallen buildings and damaged structures.

Khard and Dini were waiting for them in the Monitor building, and Dini got right down to it. "It's hopeless," he said. "It's a miracle there were no fatalities. I can assure you that another, maybe, thirty seconds, and there would have been. But we have tons of injuries, at least half the population. Most of our supplies are in ruins. Our hydroponics farms are destroyed. The grain is incinerated. Even our subspace communications facilities are destroyed. The only means of contacting help is on the ships at the landing strip, and those are short range, far less powerful. Who knows how long it would take for a message bouncing around through subspace transmission to reach someone."

"My associate has never been one for overt optimism," said Khard, "but I am forced to agree with him in this instance. As of this point, the colony is uninhabitable. If we don't get our injured and dying attended to soon, we're going to wind up with a lot of fatalities."

"And that includes your Professor Trump," said Dini.

"What is your best suggestion?" asked Worf.

"We get our people the heck off of here," Dini told him. "We have enough ships to transport colonists off. Get them to safe haven. But . . ."

He paused, and Soleta was easily able to fill in the gap. "But there's not enough room to get everyone off the planet. Some are going to have to stay behind."

"We're short room for about nine people," said Dini. "Nine people will have to stay behind. I'll be one of them, of course."

"No," said Worf firmly. "You are their leader. They will need you."

"A captain goes down with his ship."

"You are not a captain, Mr. Dini," Worf said. "Nor is this a sinking ship. This is a planet, those are colonists, and they have far greater need of you than a ruined colony site does."

"He's right," said K'Ehleyr. "And the same argument applies to you, Khard." She paused. "Nine people, eh? Very well. I, Gowr, and Kodash will stay here and await subsequent rescue. That is three."

Worf slowly turned and looked at the rest of the Dream Team. Their gazes were fixed on him, and for a moment he couldn't read their thoughts. But then Soleta slowly nodded, and the others, picking up on it, nodded as well. He felt a tremendous flash of pride.

"My people will stay behind as well," said Worf. "That makes eight. Will eight suffice, Mr. Dini?"

"But this isn't fair to you!" protested Dini. "We should—we should do it some other way. Draw straws or . . ."

"I see no advantage to some random means of designating," Soleta said. "As a group of colonists you arrived, and as a group you should depart. Just as we follow the same credo. We are qualified, and we are trained in survival. Your people are farmers. Scientists. Colonists. We, on the other hand, are Starfleet."

"And we are trained as warriors," said Gowr. "No chance drawing of straws can possibly surpass the simple logic that dictates we should be the ones who stay."

"The only question that remains is, once again, Mr. Dini, will eight suffice?" asked Worf.

Dini sighed. "In a pinch, I suppose. The additional weight will make lift-off a little trickier, but we should be able to manage."

"All right, then," said Worf. "It's settled. Draw your people together. The sooner you have departed, the better for all of you and the better your chances."

The colonists were loading themselves into the various shuttles. Everyone was traveling light, because no one wanted to bring surplus weight, and most of their belongings had been destroyed anyway.

The cadets and K'Ehleyr watched as Trump was brought past on a stretcher. He had been unconscious until that moment, but now his eyes started to flutter open. Worf and K'Ehleyr went over to him, and he looked up at them, not entirely comprehending where he was.

"Do not try to talk, sir," Worf told him as they walked alongside him toward the shuttle. "You have been injured. You will be attended to."

Trump barely glanced at him. Instead he looked at K'Ehleyr. Through cracked and bleeding lips he whispered, "You're . . . all right?"

"Yes," she said. "Thanks to you, I am fine."

"Good." His voice was barely audible. "When Alexander Trump saves 'em, they stay saved."

"I shall remember you, Alexander Trump," she said. "Heal quickly."

He tried to smile, but did not succeed. Instead his head lolled back and, for just a moment, Worf feared that he was dead. But then he saw the slow, if unsteady, rise and fall of his chest, and Worf knew that, for the moment at least, Alexander Trump was still among the living.

Dini and Khard walked over to the two groups who had chosen to remain behind.

"All right, listen up," said Dini. "The East Quad residence hall is intact, so you won't have any problem with shelter. Likewise with energy needs. The thing you've got going for you is that there's only a few of you. The generator is jerry-rigged and emergency food rations are low. But your energy requirements will be minimal, and since there's so few of you, there's more than enough food to last you for a few weeks."

"No problem then with basic survival," said Zak confidently.

"Oh, there is a basic problem, Brikar," Khard said. He gestured toward the ships. "We are operating under the assumption that the vessels were spared because the attackers wanted to be able to utilize them. There is, however, another possibility."

"A very logical one," Soleta said. "That possibility being that the attackers left the vessels intact because they wished the colonists to leave. If that were the case . . ." she trailed off.

"Then much of this has been arranged," Worf realized. "And if that *is* the case, then our greatest problem is not housing or food, but guarding against whatever plan the attackers may have set in motion."

"Nonsense," said Kodash confidently. "They assaulted us and we emerged victorious."

K'Ehleyr ignored him as she turned to Khard and said, "We will act in a matter befitting Klingon warriors—"

"And Starfleet personnel," Worf added.

Khard looked at the three Klingons. "You do honor to your empire. For this act of self-sacrifice and bravery, you will always be remembered."

Tania sidled over to Worf and said in a low, slightly nervous voice, "Why are they talking about us like we're in the past tense! I mean, we *are* going to be okay, right?"

K'Ehleyr, having overheard, turned and said in a bit of a superior tone, "There is risk involved in every stage of life. Certainly you understand that."

"Of course I understand that," retorted Tania. "It's just that—" And then she looked at Worf, watching her carefully, and suddenly she decided that a better course of action would be to keep her mouth shut. So instead she simply said, "Whatever risk is necessary to ensure the safety of others is one I will gladly take."

"Well spoken," said Khard.

Tania fought the urge to stick her tongue out at K'Ehleyr.

"All right, then," said Dini. "The only thing left to say is—good fortune, cadets. Good fortune, friend

109

Klingons. This will, with any luck, be only a brief test of your endurance. A week, two, at most.''

He turned and headed for the shuttles. Khard paused only long enough to toss off a final salute to them, and then he headed off as well.

One by one the shuttles lifted into the air, the wind roaring from the engines, and then they hurtled skyward. The last remaining inhabitants of Dantar IV stood there and watched them until the shuttles had dwindled to mere specks on the horizon.

TO BE CONTINUED

About the Author

PETER DAVID is a prolific author, having written in the past several years nearly two dozen novels and hundreds of comic books, including issues of such titles as *The Incredible Hulk, Spider-Man, Star Trek, X-Factor, The Atlantis Chronicles, Wolverine,* and *The Phantom.* He has written several popular *Star Trek: The Next Generation* novels, including *Imzadi, Strike Zone, A Rock and a Hard Place, Vendetta,* and *Q-in-Law,* the latter three spending a combined three months on the *New York Times* bestsellers list. His other *Star Trek* novels include *The Rift* and *Star Trek: Deep Space Nine: The Siege.*

His other novels include *Knight Life* (a satirical fantasy in which King Arthur returns to contemporary New York and runs for mayor), *Howling Mad* (a send-up of the werewolf legend), the *Psi-Man* and *Photon* adventure series, and novelizations of "The Return of the Swamp Thing" and "The Rocketeer." He also writes a weekly column, "But I Digress . . ." for *The Comic Buyers Guide.*

Peter is a longtime New York resident, with his wife of sixteen years, Myra (whom he met at a Star Trek convention), and their three children: Shana, Guinevere, and Ariel.

About the Illustrator

Rocketed to Earth as an infant, JAMES FRY escaped the destruction of his home planet and grew to adulthood in Brooklyn, New York. After leaving Dartmouth College in 1979 he spent considerable time at the offices of New York Telephone and Merrill Lynch. In 1984, seduced by the irresistible combination of insane deadlines and crippling poverty, he embarked on a career as a freelance illustrator. James has created numerous characters and stress-related illnesses at both Marvel Comics and DC Comics. His greatest unfulfilled ambition is to get one full night of guilt-free sleep.